WHETHER WE ARE MENDED

WHETHER WE ARE MENDED

THREE LOVE STORIES BY
PERRY SLAUGHTER

SINISTER REGARD
New York
2015

TABLE OF CONTENTS

For the Bard

WHETHER WE ARE MENDED

—sting, testing, one, two, three. *[Distant echoes of gunfire, angry voices, keening wind.]* My feedback monitors aren't working, and I can't tell whether or not my throat mike has been damaged, so I have no idea if this'll turn out. Still, I have to try. *[Beneath all, around all, slow breathing and the muted beating of a heart.]* I'm filing this under Personal Memoranda, Entry Number 379, 4 December 2756. It's some time in the early hours of the local New Year. And ... commence.

[The shifting of dust and small rubble, close at hand.] Well, I'm dying, but it remains to be seen whether or not I make it all the way to actual *death*. I've been shot in the face, my chest is laid open, and my legs are pinned beneath a ton of debris, but they'll probably still find a way to put me back together again. *[Moist cough.]* I've killed a lot of people in my day, but Death himself has always been a stranger to me. Maybe I've been too profitable a servant for Him to spare....

Whatever the reason, I feel compelled—though I've never felt compulsion in anything before—to commit the events of the past hour to wire. The nanowire spool, no bigger than a hangnail, is locked deep within my abdominal armor, somewhere in the vicinity of my spleen. Fitting *[chuckle]*, that I vent my spleen into my spleen.... *[Another chuckle, followed by severe coughing and ragged breaths.]* Zounds. I shouldn't try to amuse myself like that. If only I didn't regard humor as such a novelty....

I'm dictating this, as always, from the main spaceport in Calpurnia, capital city of the province Belatria, on Tau Ceti IV, a planet the locals call Lucern. Tonight, however, the spaceport is partially demolished, and in the streets I hear the death rattle of a doomed Revolution—one that might have succeeded if only my comrades and I been invited to take part. Within the hour, the Conglomerate strike force will arrive. There'll be fresh soldiers to mop up the few freedom fighters who've not fled the city. There'll be medics to evaluate me for recycling—and to disable my life support unit should that prove unfeasible, though that's almost to much to hope for. *[Deep, unsteady sigh.]* One way or another, There'll be an ending to this story. If it ends with my death, I'll owe it to Miranda Maria Montego.

I was working what we call the "log jam," overseeing the transfer of biafra wood to the hold of the *Charon's Ferry*, when I saw her for the first time. *[Respiration increasing slightly, heartbeat quickening.]* I can see her now, as if for the first time, as the wire replays on the cracked and melted inner surface of the visor that passes for my eyes. The pain I feel becomes all the more bittersweet each time I rewind to watch her enter the hangar, because she fired the shots that destroyed my face.

It was an hour 'til the New Year. A crowd like none I'd seen since the Biafra Rebellion had poured into the hangar. These people only wanted passage off Tau Ceti IV, and we'd been told we had nothing to fear from the rebels, but I couldn't help recalling that crowd of five Standard years before, the one that had wanted our blood, and I couldn't help the uneasiness that was building inside me. A flimsy force-cordon, through which Madman was admitting a slow trickle of passengers, was all that held this crowd back from the massive shuttle, but it would never hold against a riot. My concern was not for our safety, but for fear of reprisals against the province by the Conglomerate, whose ambassador was preparing to address the continent two thousand klicks to the east. That would ruin any chances we had of ever living ordinary lives among these people. *[A far-off explosion, and the patter of falling bits of debris.]* Unfortunately, I now know that that was never part of the plan.

The stern, familiar voice of Enid Bartollem helped me concentrate on my job, helped soothe me. Her unseeing face looked down on the crowd from holomonitors scattered throughout the hangar, brought to us by tight-beam relay from Netherheim, a planet circling the star HR 5568, which was—well, not our *home*, but where the Conglomerate had grown us and raised us and promised us all the pleasures that normal people take for granted. "Subaltern Kerr could not be reached for comment," Enid was saying. "In other news, talks are scheduled to resume tomorrow between Interior Director Arvin Rudd and leaders of the exiled Decentralization Party. Sources close to the Director say that terrorism will be a major item on the morning's agenda. Political correspondent Harrison Wertico in New Prague has more."

In a way, I miss Netherheim. I don't *love* it, but at least we weren't hated there.

As I slowly patrolled the apron, a line of obsidian-black crates drifted from the storeroom to the shuttle's hold and the back again on the invisible antigravitational track, endlessly. The crates were rectangular, as high and wide as coffins but half again as long. They approached loaded with wood, and returned again empty. I kept half my visuals trained on the loading operation, half on the crowd.

And then she appeared, seventy meters away, at the gate from the outer terminal.

It was her hair that first caught my eye across that sea of people, scintillating with interworked optical fibers that dissolved through one brilliant hue after another, but it was her face that arrested my gaze. I'd seen that face before, but a quickscan of my memory turn up no identification. I've since realized that this is the common sort of experience people refer to as *déjà vu*, but at the time I was puzzled, disturbed, and intrigued.

Buzz was working the gate, checking tickets and travel papers, and I suddenly wished I hadn't traded duties with him that night. I stepped carefully between two of the drifting crates, nearly tripping when my bad leg didn't clear the antigrav field. The leg slows me down, but I've never had it fixed, because that would strip me of a measure of my individuality. "Anything wrong, Lurch?" said Bullseye's level voice in my ear.

I tongued my throat mike and spoke with my mouth closed as I resumed a slow patrol. "No. I'm just restless." I turned my back to the crowd, stretching my arms in a such a way as to draw attention to the photon rifle slung over my shoulder. It was part of the show-of-force psychology they'd taught us on Netherheim. "There are four of us here to hold off—what, four or five hundred people?"

Bullseye was circulating through the crowd in a lazy figure-eight. A head taller than most of the crowd, like all of us, he grinned at me from beneath his jet-black visor. "Those are hardly fair odds," he said. "For them." Pleasure in violence was one of the few emotions bred into us, and Bullseye had received more than his share of those genes, which is why he led our squad. "But this bunch won't give us any trouble."

"Probably right," I said.

Bullseye started to say something else, but I shut him out and trained my directional pickup across the crowd. The girl, no more than twenty in Standard years, stood just inside the gate, arms folded and full lips pursed impatiently. Buzz was speaking to her: "Ticket, please, miss?"

The girl's head snapped to her left, hair whipping around in a flash of haughty white light, brow knotted and eyes mere slits. She shot utter contempt at poor Buzz in that brief moment, then resumed her dead-ahead stare. I heard the telltale vibration of servomechanisms that meant Buzz was out of his depth. "Miss," he said steadily, despite the buzz, "must see ticket and emigration papers before you get through."

The girl ignored him, her taut face turning to the nearest holomonitor. "It's currently five minutes to the hour of twenty-one, Galactic Standard Time," said Enid Bartollem, "on this first day of November, 2727. We're glad to have you with us this evening, especially our viewers on Tau Ceti IV, who won't be seeing this until approximately December fourth, 2756, which corresponds to the thirty-second of Disettici on their local calendar, the last day of their year 130. A happy New Year to all—"

"Miss..."

The girl looked at Buzz and said sharply, "I'm not going to Netherheim."

"Pay her no mind, youngster," said a voice like the scratch of an ancient quill pen on parchment. The girl blew out her breath and stared at the high ceiling as a very old man with a bushy white mustache hobbled through the gate, wheezing like wind through dry leaves. I could still see shades of the stout man he once had been, but the years had wrought an insidious erosion on him. Still, when he leaned against the gate and held up an encoded square of silicon, triumph blazed brightly in his ice-blue eyes. "Her ticket's right here. She's *going* to Netherheim." His clothes were of a civilian cut, but his cap was from the Belatrian army. "Where's that precious boyfriend of yours?" he whispered to the girl. "Couldn't take a break from the Revolution?"

"Shut up," she said.

Buzz accepted the ticket from the old man and inserted it into his handheld encoder/decoder. "Name?" he said.

The girl just stared at the ceiling. "I'm not going."

"Miranda Maria Montego," said the old man, ignoring the girl.

She shook her head and a red glow suffused the fiber optics in her hair. "Grandpa, I'm not going."

"Age?" Buzz said, beginning again to buzz.

"Twelve, going on thirteen," said the old man.

"Impossible," I muttered to myself, but, like most men observing an attractive woman, my higher faculties weren't completely engaged.

"*Standard* age," Buzz said.

Of course!

"Seventeen," said the girl called Miranda, tapping her fingers impatiently on the wall against which she leaned, arms folded across her abdomen. She had cut off her grandfather's reply, which, judging from his sour expression, would have been acid. The old man chewed his mustache and eyed her with a sideways scowl. She shot him a cold glare and added, "Going on eighteen."

Colored lights blinked festively beneath the old man's shirt.

"Behaving more like eight," sneered a mordant, nasal voice that well, but not perfectly, imitated human vocal patterns. "That's eleven Standard." I realized then that the girl's grandfather was fitted with a life-support unit. The processor was installed in his chest, where it could monitor vital signs and deliver nanomeds to his bloodstream. This unit was obviously top-of-the-line, wired not only for speech but also for intelligence, which meant either that the old man's finances were in healthy condition or that he had one hell of a benefits package. *[Thrumming tremor—shock wave of another distant explosion.]* Not up to par with mine, of course, but the best you could get on Tau Ceti IV. "These are her salad days, when she is yet green in judgment."

Miranda shook her fist in the direction of the old man's chest, nostrils flared. "You stay out of this, you big-mouthed piece of scrap."

"I am that I am," said the machine, "and they that level at my abuses reckon up their own."

She stepped away from the wall. "Why, you—"

A pattern of red lights strobed under the old man's shirt. "You lay a hand on me and Grandpa *dies*, little girl."

The buzz from my brother-in-arms was like the sympathetic vibration of a plate-glass window when a large craft flies overhead. People outside the gates were complaining for the line to get moving, and suddenly Buzz's rifle was in his hands, waving at the space between grandfather and granddaughter. "No time for this, people," he said, his voice pitched higher than normal. "Shuttle leaves in under forty minutes—dozens of travelers still to process. Now, cooperate or leave, your choice."

"I was just kidding," said the life-support machine softly, but the nearby onlookers had fallen silent. The general din did not diminish, however, for Buzz had not been as loud or obtrusive as, say, Madman would have been in the same situation.

Into this island of quiet poured Enid Bartollem's ubiquitous voice: "Ambassador Heyekassel and his diplomatic mission, you will remember, left Netherheim two months ago for Tau Ceti IV. By the time this broadcast reaches our viewers there, if all has gone according to plan, Heyekassel should have arrived and begun talks for the terms of that planet's annexation by the Conglomerate. Interim troops were dispatched five years ago, of course, to establish a Conglomerate presence and to set the appropriate atmosphere for the talks. Let us at Universal Broadcasting be the first to welcome you to our number, Tau Ceti IV. We're glad to have you with us. That's all for this evening. For UBS, this is Enid Bartollem. Happy holidays."

"Lucern," said the old man quietly through clenched teeth, looking toward the rifle but not seeming to see it. His eyes glittered like chunks of precious stone. "This planet is called Lucern, and that girl is *twelve* years old." His breath came shallow and harsh. He put a hand to his heart.

"Now look what you've done," said the life-support machine, and I could not tell whether he spoke to Buzz or to Miranda. The old man fell against the wall, grasping his chest and squeezing shut his eyes. "Ouch! He's on the brink of myocardial infarction, thanks to all your damned sound and fury!"

The crowd faded back uncertainly, Buzz's rifle wavered, and Miranda threw an arm around her grandfather's shoulder. Distress blurred the lines of her face; sparks danced like fireflies in her hair. "He's not going to die, is he, Les?"

"He'd better not," said the life-support machine, "or I'm out of a job." The old man's weight had pulled Miranda half off balance, and she lowered him carefully into a sitting position against the wall. "Great. He's got ectopic foci springing up like mushrooms all over his cardiac tissue. Now cracks a noble heart, if ever I saw one. Let go of him."

The girl straightened and backed away. The lights under the old man's shirt blinked like the eyes of hungry predators. Electricity cracked like the snap of a giant whip, and the old man's body bucked and jumped. A second jolt slammed through his chest, rocking his head against the wall, and his eyelids fluttered like leaves trembling in a breeze.

The crowd swirled, eddied, and parted as Bullseye flowed dispassionately through it. He emerged at Buzz's side. "Is everything okay here?"

Buzz looked down at the rifle in his hands as if in surprise and shouldered it hastily. His low vibrato was like a pale echo of the electric shocks Les had delivered to the old man's heart. "Gentleman there was having a heart attack," said Buzz. "Life-support unit saved him, looks like. Seems to be all right now."

Miranda was helping her grandfather to his feet. He looked around in some confusion. "Try to keep things under control," said Bullseye, melting back into the crowd.

"What happened, Les?" asked the old man.

"Localized necrosis of the heart. It played havoc with your sinoatrial node until I zapped away the dogs of fibrillation. Then I'm afraid I had to juice you up with Secret Sauce Number Seven to get you back on your feet."

"Oh boy, my favorite," said the old man dryly.

"Yes sir," the machine went on, "you've been snatched once more from the jaws of death, stuffed back into this mortal coil, another hour to strut and fret upon the stage—"

"What brought it on?" asked the man impatiently.

"Directly, a thrombus or an embolus. Indirectly ... well ... backtalk, I'd say. How sharper than a serpent's tooth—"

The old man shrugged off his granddaughter's supporting arm, looking at the ground. "Brat," he muttered.

Miranda stood with her hands on her hips as the old man shuffled a few paces away, outrage dissolving on her face to hurt disbelief. "Old traitor," she murmured.

"Miss Montego?" said Buzz cautiously.

Small droplets of moisture swelled in the corners of her eyes. She blinked fiercely, but one tear escaped to skitter down the smooth slope of her cheek. She wiped it brusquely away with the back of her hand. "Yeah?"

"May we..."

"Sure," she said lifelessly. Her hair had dimmed to near light-lessness.

"Thank you. Standard date of birth?"

"14 February 2739."

"Birthplace?"

"Sarocco, Belatria."

Ah, Sarocco. The land of the trees. Knowing that, I could identify one of the qualities that clung to her like a mist—earthiness, a word that persists despite mass migrations away from that planet. Sarocco lies five hundred klicks to the northwest, far beyond the River Regalia, the farthest I've ever been able to venture from this spaceport. There, nestled into the foothills of a jagged spur of the Christicus range, flourish the biafra firs that provide an economic base for all the land west of the mountains, a trade far more beneficent than the rapacious mining of silicon dioxide in the eastern lands of Meridia and Vesper. The burgundy-hued wood of the biafra, as dark as overripe cherries, is greatly prized offworld and fetches a handsome price—but the people who cultivate and fell those great trees are simple folk who nonetheless seem more *real* to me than most who have passed through this terminus. It is as though they are a part of nature, not an intrusion on it, privy to some great secret that leaves the rest of us dark-ridden.

The Conglomerate promised us natural lives on this great world after its annexation *[a soft choking sound]*, and Sarocco is the place I've always pictured as my future home. Rolling green hills, mist-shrouded valleys, ancient and wise towering trees, the stern majesty of the Christicus Mountains rising just beyond reach—close to things that are living, and far away from the pervasiveness of the technology that made and sustains us. Possibly even a family, they say, and the woman I always picture in my waking dreams so much resembles—

I could only stare at her in amazement when the realization hit. Miranda Maria Montego could have been a sister to the idealized woman I always saw in my fantasies as my wife.

"Orphaned, I see," said Buzz, peering at the small display in his hand.

The corner of the girl's compressed mouth quirked slightly. "When I was nine. Thirteen Standard."

"Grandfather is legal guardian, correct?"

Her lower lip trembled. "Yes."

"Fine. Purpose of trip?"

Her eyes flicked toward the old man. With obvious effort she said, "To attend the Netherheim Academy."

Buzz looked up. "Just under the wire. Barely make it before you're eighteen." He looked down again when she did nothing but stare straight ahead. "But you'll make it. Local branch approval is in order, as is consent of guardian. Inoculations up-to-date, physical condition satisfactory, visa current—all ready to go." He touched a small button on the display, which added his stamp of approval to the documents. He handed the silicon ticket back to Miranda. "Netherheim is not such a bad place."

The girl pocketed her ticket with surly resignation. "What do you know?" she softly spat, turning into the murmuring crowd. "Imperialist assassin."

"Soft!" said Les to the old man. "She made it through. Let's into the breach again."

With a start Miranda's grandfather raised his head, saw her disappearing, and began to hobble into the throng. "One minute," said Buzz, laying a hand on his shoulder. The old man winced, and the travelers outside the gate groaned impatiently. "Have a ticket?"

In annoyance the old man looked over his shoulder. "*I'm* not going to Netherheim," he said through twisted lips. An unsteady finger thrust toward the girl, who stood some distance away in the press of bodies, watching. "I'm just here to see that *that* young bundle of joy gets on *that* shuttle and gets off this planet."

"Need visitor's pass to enter boarding area. Have one?"

"Listen, youngster, she gave us the slip last time we were here, all because of a hardnose like you." I smiled. That would be Cudgel, whose squad worked the alternate shift. "I won't make it through this a third time."

"And that's no lie," said Les. "I've got this dude so strung out on stimulants and vasodilators that Old Man Death is just a-champin' at the bit for a chance to sink his teeth into all that chemical ecstasy. Listen, buddy, there's a tide in the affairs of men, and it leads on to fortune when taken at the flood."

"*You* listen," said Buzz, and the effort it took for him to squelch his subsonics registered on his face. "Can issue visitor's passes right here. Don't need to bribe me."

"You block, you stone, you worse than senseless thing!" shouted Les, blinking blue and orange. "That wasn't a bribe! It was a literary allusion!"

"Give me your name, sir."

The old man breathed deeply. "Okay, okay," he said. "Maximo Montego."

Buzz plugged a blank ticket into the 'coder, then spoke the old man's name into it. "Standard age?"

"Fifty-eight."

"You wish." Buzz waited.

Maximo stared intently into the middle distance. The corners of his mouth quivered on the edge of dissolution. At last he spat the number out, like a gobbet of phlegm: "Eighty-one."

Buzz brought the display close to his visor. He looked at the old man. "Your middle name Mafra?"

"A rose by any other name would smell the same," said Les.

"Yes, it is," said Maximo with resignation.

The buzz slipped beyond Buzz's conscious control. "Sir ... Mr. Montego ... sorry, but cannot issue your pass. Says here you are a known revolutionary subversive."

"I could have told you what it *says* myself, but what it *says* isn't right. I'm not into that foolishness anymore. I should have been reclassified when you buffoons took over."

"Mr. Montego, blacklists are kept quite—"

"Whoever keeps up the blacklists doesn't know his butt from a hole in the ground, if you ask me."

Buzz, sadly, has always been something of a wild card. His limits were rather hard to predict, and now he'd reached the end of his tether. "Losing patience, sir. Will. You. Please. Leave."

He said these words with such sudden rigidity and barely re-strained force that the old man stood paralyzed, like a mesmer-ized rat awaiting the strike of a viper. The life-support machine was silent. Buzz stood like a tightly coiled spring, ready to explode at the least provocation.

But Miranda, still watching, turned her back on the scene with such an air of triumph and relief that I could not help but tongue my throat mike. "Buzz? This is Lurch."

"What do you want?" he said aloud, too keyed up to subvocalize.

"You've got discretionary power over the issuance of visitor's passes."

"So? Sticking your nose in my business."

"Issue the man a pass. He's harmless enough, and he's only trying to do what he considers his duty."

Buzz turned to face me across the seventy meters of intervening people. "What about *my* duty, Lurch? Start handing out passes to every sorry old joker who comes through that gate, and what happens? Never get rid of them! They—"

"Buzz," I said with a deprecating moue, "you're holding up your travelers and making an unpleasant scene. I'll take full responsibility for whatever happens should our elderly friend get out of hand. Now, will you just come down from your high horse and issue the man a pass?"

Buzz pressed his lips together and for a moment stood stolid. "Don't understand you at all," he murmured subvocally, then spread his arms low as if in prelude to a mocking bow. "All right. Fine. But on *your* head, you understand?"

"All right, fine," I said, and Buzz began speaking into his 'coder.

Why I came to the old man's defense may require some explanation. The Conglomerate would have its soldier-slaves, believe that only on a planet under its own dominion can we live at peace with true humans. That's how they ensure our loyalty. After all, we're not human, despite our genes. We're no more than cultured protoplasm grown inside humanoid sheaths, and normal people fear and hate us, as the Biafra Rebellion, a needlessly violent welcoming party from the first week of our occupation, made perfectly clear. Still, nothing's so simple as the Conglomerate would like to make it.

From our first moments here, I've been convinced that a truer peace could be achieved through understanding. To that end I've become a student of human behavior. I've read all the treatises, from Freud and Jung and Skinner right through Kirchhoefer and Oudomvidlay and Xaiz, but I've found the race's literary offerings more useful, with emphasis on the writings of Shakespeare, who first sparked in me the notion that I could learn through observation and inference. *[Several sets of footsteps approach, pounding rhythmically. Voices bark harsh orders.]* During the course of this transitional period between planetary self-government and Conglomerate annexation, I've filled three hundred seventy-eight of these reports with the instances typical human behavior I've witnessed in this very hangar.

One thing I have learned in the course of my observations is that people are rarely more themselves than when they are angry. *[The footsteps pass by, some distance away, and slowly fade out.]* Anger provides the surest conduit to the depths of the soul, for its heat scours away all the encrusted niceties that build up as one travels through society. The thing that remains is red and raw, like a bared nerve that shrieks at the smallest stimulus. People will let slip things in anger that they would otherwise reveal only under torture.

My reasoning was simple. I wanted to learn more about Miranda, so I had to keep her angry. That meant keeping her near her grandfather, which in turn meant getting him through the gate. I needed to know how her face had come to invade my dreams.

Maximo accepted his pass without question and hobbled away from Buzz as quickly as he could, as if fearful that the boon would be taken back. "I'll never understand those miscreant cyborgs," he said with a scowl. "They call themselves soldiers? Hah. I could show them a few things about soldiering."

"So could I," said Les, "but they're all buried in that cemetery we always visit."

The old man, who had pushed his way feebly into the crowd, paused to peer about. With all the milling people I couldn't always keep him in sight, but I kept my pickup trained in his general direction. "Those were all good men," he said, and suddenly he sounded much older than even eighty-one. "That snake Romulus Valenti has everyone believing that they weren't, even my own granddaughter, but I was there"—his voice resolved into a sharp hiss—"and they were *good men*."

"I know." The lights winked a in consoling pattern of light blue, like the ripples on a pond. "The good that men do is oft interred with their bones."

"But it wasn't. That's the point." Maximo gestured like a lecturer, and the people close at hand politely ignored this old man who talked to himself. "You wouldn't remember, but they were buried for nearly forty-three years before anyone questioned their heroism—forty-three solid Lucernian *years*, none of this Galactic Standard garbage. They paved the way for the Conciliation. It's not their fault if the Meridians called in the Conglomerate behind our backs. Les, the stories I could tell you about that bunch..."

"Unfortunately, they all end with the same plot—a burial plot."

The old man smiled, the crowd swirling about him like the mists of time. "I sure miss them. You know, we'd place bets on every skirmish, but whoever took the pot always ended up blowing it on drinks for the rest of us. Can't wait to see those guys again..."

"My prediction is you won't have to wait too long, Max. Max?"

His blue eyes were rheumy, as if the ice of a few minutes before were melting. Maximo rocked slowly back on his heels. Urgent red light flashed from his chest. "Wha—? Les?" He caught his balance and shook his head. "Am I okay?"

"No, and how have you the leisure to be sick in such a justling time? Sauce Number Seven's losing its effectiveness, so I've had to supplement it with Thirteen."

The watery eyes were refreezing even as I watched, and the old man's head cocked this way and that in the manner of a small bird. With as much medication as he had no doubt absorbed, it was a miracle he was still alive. "It's pretty bad, then, eh?"

"This is another nail in your coffin. I don't think your body's going to be able to take much more."

Maximo slapped his hands together and rubbed them eagerly. "With any luck, it won't have to. I see Miranda."

She stood near the cordon, to my side of Madman's checkpoint, hair suffused with a pale blue glow, studying a small display she held in her hand. Her head nodded slightly from moment to moment, as if she were checking off items from a mental list, and when the inventory was complete her gaze shifted to the *Charon's Ferry*, which she faced from a short distance behind that pitifully fragile force-cordon. As the old man threaded, weaved, and lunged his way toward her through the crowd, the holomonitors, which were now receiving planetary news from Meridia, went mute, and a scratchy, bored voice echoed across the hangar:

"Ladies and gentlemen, boarding for Flight 1732 of the shuttle *Charon's Ferry* will end in fifteen minutes, at 19:39. To ensure that our passengers have ample time to reach their seats before the antigravitational field is activated, we would ask that all visitors complete their farewells as quickly as possible. Departure will be at precisely 19:49, when the solar tide is most in our favor. The shuttle will rendezvous at 8:14 tomorrow morning with the geosynchronous space station *Tyrol*, for transfer of passengers and cargo to the starliner *Godspeed*—"

Miranda, distracted only briefly by the announcement, checked her display once more. Her gaze then followed the contoured lines of the shuttle until it swept onto the loading apron and brushed against me. I flinched involuntarily, as if a jet of cold air had sprayed across my face. A nimbus of crackling yellow surrounded her face, and our eyes met for the first of two times that night. Though she couldn't see mine, veiled as they were behind a sheath of glasticene, hers burned into me like drilling lasers laying bare unrefined ore, and for a moment I understood what it would be like to wear my flesh exposed and unprotected. I felt naked and vulnerable before her, which made no sense, for what fueled the heat of her gaze was hatred, and I had stood unflinching before hatred a hundred times before.

"—recent developments in massless acceleration," the announcement went on, "the *Godspeed* will reach a velocity of within a millionth part of the speed of light in three and a half days. Due to relativistic effects, the twenty-nine-year journey will pass for the travelers in just four to five subjective weeks. We will dock with the space station *Netherview* sometime in the early days of 2786, where all immigrants will receive corrected birthdates to correspond with their biological ages—"

Though we stared at each other for only a few seconds, some phantom reverse effect of relativity stretched the time to its asymptotic limit, until I almost believed I had never been anything but a particle buffeted by the harsh lines of force that radiated from her eyes. And then suddenly her gaze shifted, and I came to myself like a sleeper who, emerging from a dream that seemed to last an hour, finds that only a moment has elapsed. The long black crates that were my stewardship now occupied her attention. Her eyes followed one on its lazy circuit from the storeroom to the shuttle and back. She looked down at the display, then back at the crates. Her lips moved slightly, as if she were committing some cryptic message to memory. So intent was she on this exercise, she didn't notice the old man until he was peering over her shoulder.

"Whatcha got there, girl?" he said brightly.

With a start she turned. "Oh, great," she muttered. Lavender trails flickered through her hair. "How did you get in here?"

"I asked my question first. What is it? Looks like some kind of schematic diagram."

"Oh," she said as she slipped the display into a spacious pocket, "well, it's a ... it lets me preselect my seat on the shuttle. I got it from the ticket agent. Don't you remember?"

Maximo shook his head with a hard grimace. "Actually, no."

"Yeah, well, that doesn't surprise me. You've forgotten a lot in the last few years." She zipped the pocket shut. "Excuse me, Grandpa. I need to use the ladies' room."

The old man gripped her arm lightly, still shaking his head, and the grimace became a conspiratorial smile. "I haven't forgotten *that* trick yet, young lady. You won't get away so easily this time."

She shrugged. "It was worth a try," she said dryly. "I guess it was pretty foolish of me to think I could outfox an old snake like you."

Les chuckled, a cackle that sounded evil coming from a machine. "I'd rather have a fool to make me merry than experience to make me sad."

"Get lost," she said. "Just for the record, Grandpa, I want you to know it's pretty cold of you to make me leave tonight of all nights."

"Whose fault is that?" said Maximo. "You could have left as early as last Quattordici, but you had to keep dragging your heels and putting it off. And it's not every day we can make a trip clear to Calpurnia."

"But I want to be home for the—" She broke off in mid-sentence, waving her hand as to dismiss the thought.

"For the what? The holidays? Since when have you ever cared about the holidays?"

"I want to see the fireworks tonight," she grumbled. "Besides, Christmas falls on Conciliation Day this year. That won't happen again for over a century."

"So take a nice long relativistic trip when you graduate," Les said, "and you can be here for it."

"I don't understand why you even care about Conciliation Day," said Maximo. "The treaty was a sham, even if we didn't find out for forty-two years."

Miranda shrugged free of the old man's grasp. "Ever since we *did* find out, Conciliation Day has reminded us how we were betrayed by the Meridian Alliance. It's a day for remembering who our enemies are."

"Stop. Please. You sound like one of Romulus Valenti's damned propaganda brochures."

She faced him with her hands on her hips. "Valenti's a scholar and a patriot, and he makes a lot more sense than you do."

"Come on. He's nothing but a cowardly old man and a filthy liar, and you're a fool to believe anything he says."

"Oh, yeah? Well, you've been a coward *and* a fool ever since the Rebellion."

Maximo's eyes glittered dangerously. "If you were a man I'd have you back up a statement like that with some action."

"I don't have to. Everyone knows it's true. You used to call yourself a freedom fighter, but when things went bad, you just gave up. You quit. You turned your back on everything you ever fought for. *Someone* had to take over, and Valenti was the only one with enough guts to do it."

"That's a load of bunk, girl, but even if it weren't, that fascist ratbag still wouldn't be the man for the job. *I* know. I was in the same platoon with him in the Trade Wars. I was only thirteen at the Battle of the Ellazon—"

"That's eighteen Standard, Galactic girl," whispered Les mockingly.

"—and he was fifteen, and he *deserted*. It was the decisive battle of the whole *war*, and he wasn't even *there*. All of us but him got Wooden Crosses—most of which had to be awarded posthumously, because most of those men gave their *lives* in that battle—and he's spent the rest of his life trying to live that down. I've been a war hero and a senator, but all he's ever been is a hack political writer."

"Does that make any difference? Can't a writer love his country, too?"

"Of course—anyone can—but that's not—"

"Anyone? Then why not me? Why send me away when I could fight and bring some honor back to the family name?"

Rage twisted Maximo's mouth, but Les spoke first. "By heaven, you'd think it were an easy leap to pluck bright honor from the pale-faced moon, or dive into the bottom of the deep, where fathom-line could never touch the ground, and pluck up drowned honor by the locks. It doesn't work that way, honey."

"You stupid machine. What do you know?"

"I know that you're a little more than kin to this man, and a little less than kind."

"Will you give the Shakespeare a rest? You have no idea what you're talking about, and I'm sick of hearing it."

"Oh, yeah? Well, you tread on my patience, you ungrateful, marble-hearted fiend!"

"Damn you—"

"Now *there's* a good mouth-filling oath."

I enjoyed this exchange, to be honest, for I had at last caught on to the source of the life-support machine's eloquent maxims. For me, memory, the warder of the brain, has always been a paradox; once remembered, events replay before my eyes as if I were actually there again, but my imperfect recall often requires a none-too-subtle prompt to set it in motion. Indeed, when to the sessions of sweet and silent thought I summon up remembrance of things past, I sigh the lack of many a thing I sought. *[The engine of an individual transport whines past overhead.]* I felt silly for not realizing sooner how liberally Les had borrowed from the immortal words of the Bard of Avon, but having realized it I immediately regarded him as sort of a spiritual comrade, and Miranda's criticisms stung me as sharply as they did him—or would have, if he'd had any true feelings to be hurt.

"Quiet, you two," said Maximo sharply. He took Miranda's arm again and escorted her slowly but firmly toward the queue at Madman's checkpoint. "Miranda, this world isn't like it used to be. Back when I was a boy, we had something *real* to fight for—our homes and our families and our freedom. What's at issue today is an *ideal*—who's going to govern us. There are no lives at stake, no captives to liberate, not even any trading rights to gain. A principle is all we have to fight for, and that's just not as inspiring as having a gun at your head. In fact, you ask most of your revolutionary friends what they're trying to accomplish, and they can't even give you a straight answer. They're just trying to recapture some of the glory of the past, and it can't work."

Miranda's hair flashed like the self-defense mechanism of some creature native to the jungle. "So what you're saying is that my parents—your son—died for nothing."

"That's what I've always said." Emotion choked the old man's voice like a strangler's garrote. "The Biafra Rebellion was ill-conceived and suicidal, and the sad fact of the matter is that it didn't change a thing. It was like I took every one of those people myself and dashed their brains out against a wall. Their blood is all on my hands."

"Out, damned spot—out, I say," murmured Les.

"Grandpa, I'm tired of you blaming yourself for those deaths. You didn't kill anybody—it was monsters just like these ones here. If there's nothing I can do to pay those murderers back, then my parents really did die in vain."

It was Madman to which she pointed, saying this, but I felt the bite of her anger just the same, felt it stir up times past inside of me. As I said, all I need is a prompt, and my memory can be as perfect as a falling snowflake. A face as like Miranda's as the mold is like model arose in my mind with the humor of a disquiet spirit. "What may this mean," I whispered to myself, "that thou, dead corse, again in complete steel revisitest thus the glimpses of the moon, making night hideous, and we fools of nature so horridly to shake our disposition with thoughts beyond the reaches of our souls?"

The spools of nanowire rolled back almost of their own accord, and in an instant I was five years younger and the crowd in the hangar had suddenly turned on us, drawing clubs and bludgeons from under their traveling clothes, and that haunting Miranda-face snarled at me like a wild animal as the laser-spot from my unslung rifle found the center of her throat and the photon bursts followed it just a moment later, burning through her esophagus to sever the spinal cord, and she fell with all the grace of swan cut down in flight and the spot jumped to its next target....

There's something about killing that creates for me an eternal bond with the victim, something in the eyes as that final breath is drawn that mutely gives me thanks for showing him or her the way into peace and repose. It's a journey I despair of ever making, so each traveler I help along the road becomes a precious friend to me—but none more so than that woman whose blood was the first I ever spilled, who I now knew was Miranda's mother. The face from my dreams, the strange *déjà vu*, the helplessness before the girl's hatred, I now understood. *[Debris shifts and clatters.]* By the pricking of my thumbs, I am afraid I understood it.

"Your father wanted you to leave this planet before there was another misguided Rebellion," said Maximo quietly. "On his deathbed—"

"Grandpa—"

"Let me finish. He was dying from his wounds, and when I had to tell him his Lenta was dead, he made me swear I'd get you off this planet. He wanted you at the Academy, someplace where you could learn enough to *really* help your planet."

"In your imagination. My father would never have wanted that."

"He died too soon, or he would have told you himself."

"He died too soon, so you could make up any story you wanted to."

"You lie in your throat if you say this is any other than an honest man," said Les. "If you could just taste his galvanic skin response, you'd know—"

"By the telling of it, he's made such a sinner of his memory to credit his own lie!" said Miranda. She turned a stiff back on them and began to walk away.

"Epinephrine, Les," said Maximo through clenched teeth.

"What?"

"Give me a shot of epinephrine, *now*."

"Are you crazy, Max? Do you know what that'll do to you?"

"Of course I do, but if I don't get her on that shuttle then it won't matter very much, now will it?"

Lights of all colors flickered in consternation. "Max ... oh, all right, all right. A double epinephrine on the rocks, coming right up—dry, just the way you like it. A toast to your health."

"Thank you." In the old man's eyes smoldered a slow fire. He clenched his fists, and ropy muscles quivered as they were flooded with adrenaline-rich blood. In five steps he reached his granddaughter and swung her about. His fingers dug into her upper arms with such white-knuckled force that her skin would surely bruise. "Young lady," he said in a hoarse snarl, the girl too stunned to struggle, "you have an aunt and two uncles who went to the Academy, and the only reason your father Moreno didn't follow them was because he couldn't bear to leave your grandmother and me here all alone. When he met your mother, she was practically on her way to the Academy herself, and he talked her into staying. When he was dying, he couldn't forgive himself for keeping her here, and said he'd never forgive me if I let the same thing happen to you."

"But—"

"But nothing." He dragged her forcibly back toward the

boarding queue, through a smaller but more curious throng, and her hair flashed red with distress. "No matter how much you try to fool yourself with fancy rhetoric, the real reason you want to stay is for that Tavagne boy you think you're in love with. Am I right?"

"Grandpa—" It was the plea of a frightened child.

"Do you see him here?" Maximo gestured with a free hand. "Do you? I was looking forward to meeting him, and he didn't even bother to show up! He's too busy playing revolutionary soldier to worry about the girlfriend he's never going to see again! Did you ever loan him that spool of *Julius Caesar* to read?"

"Well, yes..."

"And?"

She looked away. "He gave up before the end of the first act."

"Of course he did. Now tell me what the two of you have ever had in common with each other. Can you?"

"Benolo loves Belatria, and so do I."

"That's beautiful. I hope the three of you will be very happy." The old man pushed his way to the head of the queue. A fat lady tried to protest, but he silenced her with a murderous glare. "Youngster," he said, addressing Madman, "this here's my granddaughter." He thrust her roughly at my unbalanced comrade. "She's got a ticket, and I want her on that shuttle immediately."

Madman grinned, bending like a sinuous black reptile to study Miranda's pallid face. The reflection of her hair cast a patina of blood over his opaque visor. "You got the right idea, old man," he said, his voice like a rusted pipe. "Woman gets outta line, you gotta slap her around a little, show her who's boss." His subsequent cackle was a blood-chilling thing, even more so to me because Madman was the only one of our number who could laugh. An accident on Netherheim had lead to his recycling—brain transplanted into another body—and I have often reflected that, no matter what he may have lost in the transfer, he gained things from it that the rest of us can never understand.

Miranda turned her head. Fear disfigured her face. "Grandpa, what are you going to do when you're all alone?"

"Ask for me tomorrow and you shall find me a grave man," said Les, but I don't think she heard him.

"I won't be alone. I've got Les."

She looked past Madman at the shuttle's eerily lit hatchway. She looked back at Maximo. "Grandpa, I—"

"Go on, girl. You're holding up the line."

"But Grandpa—don't you know how much I want to stay here with—"

"This ain't no true confessions here, Miss Bleeding Heart. Let's get a move on." Madman leered like a grimacing skull, showing his perfect, bone-white teeth. "The solar tides don't wait for no broad, and neither do I." Again he cackled.

"You should forget about that Tavagne boy." With his hand the old man made little shooing motions. "Now go."

The expression that jarred her features I would have expected from a person feeling the lash of a whip. Her demeanor changed as abruptly as if a switch had been thrown, and very deliberately she fished the small encoded ticket out of her pocket and pressed it into Madman's palm. She strode through the cordon and across the apron with the finality of a soldier on a forced march to her death. I nonchalantly wandered to the edge of the loading apron, where I could see around the corner of the shuttle and into the open hatchway. A handful of loiterers, separated from me by the thin cordon, moved back like filings repulsed by a magnet. I watched as Miranda mounted the short flight of steps that led into the vessel. Just inside the hatchway she paused, turned; the lonely, pale blue light of her hair reflected from the tracks on her cheeks to turn her face into a map of forsaken rivers.

At times it lies within man's power to work magic with words. I refer not to the arcane spells and incantations of a less enlightened age, nor to the transcendent rhapsodies some poetry can work on the mind, but rather to the effect that three small words in particular can have upon the human temperament. I have seen anger softened, tears evaporated, discord banished, and deep wounds healed by the mere recitation of those words, but never have I seen a person more in need of that healing than Miranda was at that moment.

Maximo, just twenty paces away from her, seemed to sense also that something needed to be said, and that he needed to say it. "Ah, Miranda—you take care of yourself, and remember that I..." Inchoate hope brightened the girl's eyes, and I could imagine a beauteous smile bursting through those tears—sunshine and rain all at once. "I ... have children on Netherheim. You look 'em up when you get there and let 'em know I was still okay when you left."

Needless to say, those weren't the magic words. Miranda's features seemed to come apart as if the force that bound them in place had suddenly vanished. She turned without a word and disappeared into the shuttle, leaving nothing but an afterflash of yellow pain on my retinas to indicate where she had been.

"Ain't that just like a dame," said Madman, as philosophically as he was able. "If she ain't yappin' at you like a dog at a catfight, then the waterworks are goin' full blast." He giggled with more than a touch of hysteria. "Take it from me—you're better off without that one. They come twice as good for half the price."

Maximo stood where he was, staring at the empty hatchway, until the fat lady in front of whom he had earlier shoved nudged him impatiently out of her way. Madman's evil cackle tolled about him like a sounding bell. The old man seemed numb, cut off from his own feelings, and only the voice of his life-support machine could shake him from his reverie. "Parting is such sweet sorrow that I shall say goodbye 'til it be morrow."

The old man blinked his eyes, then suddenly began to tremble, with, I suppose, a delayed reaction to his massive dose of adrenaline. "I've got to sit down, Les," he said. He shuffled through the thinning crowd like a wind-up toy close to running down. He seated himself on one of a brace of wooden benches near the center of the boarding area, from which he could still see the hatchway of the *Charon's Ferry*. "Well, is that it?" he asked when the trembling had nearly passed. "Is she really gone?"

"Almost, it would seem," said Les. "And so are you."

Maximo cupped his chin in his hand. "Did you think she was acting strangely those last few minutes?"

"The lady did protest too much, methinks, but other than that—yes, I'd have to say she was."

The old man took that in slowly. "Oh, what have I done?" he moaned, his head sinking nearly to his crossed knees. "I didn't even say goodbye to her. She's on her way to another planet, Les, and I'm never going to see her again, and I didn't have the decency to say goodbye. I didn't even tell her I..." His voice sank to unintelligibility.

I could detail more of Maximo's grief, but to be honest, I find it both disturbing and deeply embarrassing to intrude upon another person's sorrow. Let me just say that the old man wept.

The boarding period was nearly over, and I let the last few crates deposit their loads in the shuttle before shutting down the operation. Each was fitted at one end with a coupler, which allowed it to dock with a special port in the side of the shuttle through which the wood was automatically transferred. The final crate docked and was relieved of its contents, but when it began its drift back to the storeroom it listed to one side with a corner scraping along the floor, as if there were an unevenly distributed load inside. It was no emergency, but as a precaution I cut the power to the system, making a mental note to check out the problem after the hangar was shut down for the night. The crate settled gently to the ground.

"With a little more than twenty minutes to the year 131," proclaimed the holomonitors, tinny crowd noises almost overwhelming the reporter's voice, "the grounds of historic Carvello Hall here in Santaglio, Meridia, are literally packed with revelers awaiting the stroke of midnight. It was on this site, overlooking the mighty Ellazon River, nearly forty-six years ago—or close to sixty-four in Standard reckoning—that Raldo Papel of Meridia and Tyrol Santamari of Belatria signed the groundbreaking Treaty of Conciliation. Tonight, within those alabaster walls, another grand meeting has been convened—"

Through the cordon Madman ushered the last of his boarding passengers, seeing them to the hatchway with a series of mocking bows and exhortations and fending off their loved ones. The steps folded in upon themselves, and the hatch swung shut with the stately grace of a prison-yard door. I ducked under the cordon. A subsonic hum rolled up through the floor and into my bones. The antigrav pad beneath the shuttle was warming up. Madman and I waved the scattered onlookers away from the cordon and then assumed our guard positions at opposite sides of the hangar. Bullseye and Buzz stood near the gate. Old Maximo on his bench lifted his head and rested his chin on his fist. He watched the shuttle with a face full of the stolid vigilance that is companion only to fatigue.

"—Ambassador Pol Heyekassel representing the Conglomerate, Premier Firenzo Illyron for the Meridian Alliance, and Governor Lem Tigliano for Belatria. Accompanying the delegation from the Meridian Alliance are representatives from each of its subsidiary states, Meridia, Vesper, Manzan, and the Island of Gondola. It is expected that at midnight Ambassador Heyekassel will ring in the New Year with an official statement of the—"

"Of the terms of our surrender," said Maximo to himself morosely.

"Annexation," said Les, correcting him.

"Surrender, annexation, it's all the same. It was over a long time ago, and there's no use fighting it now."

"Sometimes the better part of valor is discretion."

"True," he said softly. "It's a shame, but it's true. Why couldn't she realize that?"

The minutes passed quietly. In the background droned various roving newspeople, with updates on holiday festivities across the continent, but I could not spot anyone in the hangar bay who seemed to care. These were people whose loved ones were soon to streak through space at near lightspeed for twenty-nine years, aging only a matter of weeks. *[Several sudden coughs. Voice begins to deteriorate slightly.]* They would never be back, or if they were it would not be until the left-behinds had long since lain down in their graves and crumbled to dust. The only comfort for these lonely watchers was the notion that perhaps their departed might be happier as fully privileged citizens of the Conglomerate on its capital world than as its unwilling subjects on lands that had always been their own, free and clear. There would be no New Year celebration in this small corner of Calpurnia.

I had no cause for rejoicing, either. I was frustrated by the fact that the daughter of the woman from my dreams had given me

nothing but a brief lesson in revolutionary thought, when what
I had hoped for was a key to all the mysteries that had plagued
my waking life. All I had to celebrate was the hope that my
comrades and I would soon be allowed to retire to the countryside, to live out our days among the verities of nature, in bodies that with any luck would someday succumb to the sleep of
death—but if the ambassadorial entourage did not include sufficient relief soldiers, as seemed likely from the fact that no new
troops had been mentioned on the holomonitors, our contracts
just might be up for mandatory renewal. Another five years of
spaceport duty would be no call for merriment.

Soon the pad had reached full power. A widening crack appeared in the ceiling above the shuttle as the massive hangar
doors slid apart. The breath of winter bit shrewdly, a nipping
and an eager wind, and I saw the old man trembling in its chill.
The night was clear, its stars gazing down through the gap in the
ceiling like ten thousand sad eyes bright with tears. Automatic
dampers gradually eased up on the antigrav pad, and, without
ceremony or fanfare but with the grace of a rising swan, the
Charon's Ferry lifted off the ground. It plied upward through the
open gap, white as an eggshell against the black-velvet night,
snatching its pale fire from the beams of powerful searchlights
mounted on the roof of the hangar. It rose and rose, and as it
went it dwindled to a brilliant pinprick, until it was no longer
distinguishable from the stars amongst which its passengers
were soon to race. The first leg of their long journey was underway.

One by one, the onlookers unbent their craning necks, shaking their heads or wiping their eyes or muttering to one another,
and began shuffling toward the exits, off on the next leg of their
own trips through a joyless holiday season. Only Maximo stayed

where he was, eyes fastened on the sky as if he could still pick out the tiny shuttle from the midst of all those twinkling constellations. What was that expression on his face? Wistfulness? Regret? Loneliness? I couldn't tell.

"Old man not leaving, Lurch," said Buzz's voice in my head. "Your responsibility. Get rid of him."

The hangar doors were sliding shut, and the lights were dimming to the lowest level by which we could still see well enough to get around. Maximo's chest blinked in the electric-blue hue of a homing beacon. "This poor man suffered a heart attack not long ago," I said calmly. "I'd like to let him rest awhile before sending him out into the cold. Bullseye?"

"That's fine. He's not in the way of anything. Just see that he does get out eventually."

"Sure."

"Gotta get out while the gettin's good," Madman said with a cackle.

"*Your* responsibility, not mine," said Buzz pointedly.

"Yes, we've established that already. Thank you, Buzz."

As we began to police the boarding area, the old man looked away from the ceiling to stare blankly at the pre-midnight revelry in the nearby holomonitor, and then he looked at his shoes. "Seems she's really gone, Les," he said, his voice like wind through a hollow tree.

"Looks that way. Which means you're next."

Maximo's eyes grew big and round, and he absently chewed his mustache. "Yeah. I guess that's what it means."

The lights blinked in an uncertain pattern, in uncertain colors. "You still want to go through with it, don't you? You're not going to rescind my programming..."

"Oh, yeah, yeah, no. Sorry. I was just thinking about Envaline.

My wife, you know. She died back in 109, after Metello and Inverna and Midrin had all left for the Academy. I was wondering what she thinks about all this."

"Well, you can ask her before too much longer." Les paused. "You want to fly back home before we do this?"

"Huh? Oh ... no. That's too far to go. Besides, I don't think I could fight my way back out through the city tonight."

"You're probably right. It's one big party out there, and you and I are past our dancing days, that's for sure."

I performed my tasks automatically, following this conversation with rapt fascination. I had read of many suicides in Shakespeare, but never had I been fortunate enough to witness one in person. The bonds between me and those people to whom I had shown the way to dusty death were so powerful that I could scarcely imagine what it might be like to be my own guide into that mysterious netherworld. I envied old Maximo for that ultimate self-communion, and silently I wished him godspeed.

He folded his arms and sat back. He waited. "Well?"

"Well what?"

"How soon?"

"Uh, Max ... are you sure you want to go through with this? I mean, this fell sergeant, death, is strict in his arrest."

"*You're* not getting cold feet now, are you?"

"Well, no ... I just want to be sure you're making an informed choice. Once I put out thy light, thou cunningest pattern of excelling nature, I know not where is that Promethean heat that can thy light relume. That's the end, that's it, finito, kaput, end of story. You can't change your mind if you don't like it."

"Les, I've been waiting for this for a long time, and you have, too. My promise to Moreno is kept, and I just want it all to be over."

"I know, I know. It's just that—it's just that I've always been a life-*extension* system, and it's not an ea—easy thing for me to override my basic directives. But hey, for you, Max—anything. Here goes."

I don't know what kind of medication Les administered to Maximo. I *do* know that a dreamy look entered the old man's eyes, and that he leaned his head against the back of the bench with a beatific smile on his lips. He chuckled. "Les, have you ever heard the one about the golfer and the funeral procession?"

"I have, but—*kwlrk!*—I don't suppose that'll stop you from telling it again."

"Well, there's this old golfer, see, and he's on the green lining up a birdie shot when this big funeral procession goes floating by on the other side of the fence. So, the golfer stops what he's doing and takes off his hat and stands there all reverent and re-spectful while this procession goes by, and when it's gone his buddy says to him, 'Hey, I never realized you had that kind of respect for the dead,' and the golfer puts his hat back on and picks up his putter and says, 'Yeah, well, that wasn't just *any* dead person, you know. That was my wife.'"

Maximo slapped his knee then and laughed so hard that I feared he would fall off the bench and hurt himself—not that it would really have mattered at that point—and Les dutifully joined in with his own harsh, mechanical laughter. Myself, I didn't get it. I was saddened by the thought of the death of the woman in the anecdote and angered by her husband's callous disregard for what should have been a tragedy to him. I failed entirely to see anything humorous about the situation—a failure that left me very disap-pointed. The old man and the machine just laughed and laughed, more hysterically by the moment, and some time had passed be-fore I realized that Maximo's laughter had changed into crying.

"Max?" said Les. "Oh, come—come—come—come on, Max. Let not women's weapons, waterdrops, stain your man's cheeks. It can't—*brrchh!*—be that bad."

Maximo's breathing became more regular, but the tears did not cease to flow. "What are you going to do when I'm gone?" he said between great shuddering breaths.

"Though by medicine life may be pro—prolonged, yet death will seize the doctor too."

Maximo nodded, mustache quivering. "That's good," he said, "very good," and the sobbing began again.

Les cried out as if in pain. "O, that I might see—*tsskp!*—what the old wo—wo—world could say to this composed wonder of your frame! Whether we are men—men—mended, or wheth-er better they, or whether—*chrrt!*—whether revolution be the same!"

Suddenly the old man on the bench fell over onto his side, eyes closed and cheeks wet. "Miranda," he said in a voice as thin as paper, and then he was still.

The lights on his chest still blinked in agitation, however. "Good night, sweet pr—prince," said Les reverently. He made a wistful sound, like the echo of the static between the stars. "I shall not loo—look upon his like again. Nothing in his life became him like—*aggsth!*—the leaving it; he died as one that had been stud—stud—studied in his death to throw away the dearest thing he owed, as 'twere a care—*flrjk!*—careless trifle. But soft, what's here? A cup, closed in my—*whrff!*—true love's hand? Poison, I see, hath been his timeless end. O ch—ch—churl! Drunk all, and left no friendly drop to help me af—after? I will kiss thy lips. Haply some poison yet doth—*dnggp!*—hang on them to make me die with a restorative. Thy lips are war—war—warm."

In truth, the old man's lips were turning blue. I switched to infrared vision—which I rarely use, because it gives me a headache—and I realized that Maximo's blood was cycling through the life-support unit, being cooled to help preserve the body. I stooped then to pick up a scrap of litter, and my bad leg scraped along the ground with a sound like the grating of fingernails on slate.

"Yea, noise?" said Les in surprise. "Then I'll be—be—be brief. O happy dagger! This is thy sheath. There rust, and—*trsklz!*—let me die." The machine made several more sparking and sputtering noises, its lights flashing in a wild spasm of color and random patterning. Its final words, spoken aside, were: "Who—*sprtt!*—who would have thou—thou—thought the old man to have had so—so much blood in him?"

And the lights on Maximo's chest went dark.

I paused in my labors, honoring this tortured old soldier and his glib ancient with a moment of silence. The thought that such noble passings should go unreverenced I still find disagreeable, and I would like to think that these words of mine may soon attain a sympathetic ear, one who will join me in offering my most sincere respects to these newly dead. Without—*[voice suddenly cracks, and resumes more scratchy than before]*—without those brave souls who precede us into that undiscovered country from whose bourn no traveler returns, whom will we have to befriend us when we follow?

Bullseye had locked the opaque gate to the hangar bay, and we were shortly to begin our security patrol. The guards from the outer terminal were a bit behind schedule, for they should have checked in with us once their area was secure. "This is it, everyone!" shouted a jubilant reporter into a local Belatrian holocamera, and her image peered down on us excitedly from the monitors. Along with the hometown crowd, she chanted: "Ten, nine, eight, seven, six, five, four, three, two, *one!* All right! It's 131, everybody—and just *look* at those fireworks bursting over Calpurnia Square!"

I heard explosions from afar, but not faintly enough to be coming from Calpurnia Square. The camera swung up to show all of Belatria the beautiful magnesium flowers blooming in the sky, but suddenly the holomonitor I was watching, and, indeed, the entire front gate to the hangar, blew toward my comrades and me in a blinding ball of fire. It was as if the mouth of hell had gaped suddenly open and spewed all its violence at us. A twisted piece of girder struck me in the chest, throwing me a full twenty meters, and the exposed lower half of my face was peppered with flying glasticene. Still, I might have escaped mostly intact had my legs been agile enough to help me scramble out from under a teetering section of roof. When it fell, however, I was pinned to the ground.

Buzz was killed instantly in the explosion, his head torn straight from his shoulders, but I suspect he will live again if the medics arrive soon enough to preserve his brain. The chop-fallen head rolled to nearly within my reach, and were it not for the extent of my injuries I might have succumbed to the overwhelming urge I had to scoop it up and deliver Hamlet's famous eulogy to the long-dead Yorick. Madman lived, for I could hear his ravings above the clattering of debris, and I was momentarily to discover that Bullseye had a few measures of life left in him, as well.

Great chunks of roofing formed a cairn before the new, wider gateway, and four trim figures stormed smartly over it through the smoke and rising dust. Three of the revolutionaries brandished projectile weapons of local manufacture; the fourth held a stolen Conglomerate photon rifle in one hand and a small display unit in the other. They advanced cautiously, but from a corner of the hangar behind and to the right of them, from out of a gray pile of rubble, came the short and deadly sizzle of one of our own weapons. The nearest of the young men pitched forward onto his face, a broad black burn on the back of his hand-sewn khaki uniform. True to his name, Bullseye, his face and one steel-sheathed arm emerging from the rubble, began to draw a bead on the next boy-soldier, but before the laser-spot had fixed on its victim all three intruders had whirled and laid open the throats of their weapons. Bullseye's chalky face burst open in a steaming red spray, like the splitting of a ripe baccacia fruit, before it was obscured in a cloud of smoke and dust.

One of the revolutionaries kept right on firing after the others two had stopped, with tears streaking the dust on his face. The rattle of his gun and the *ping!* of ricocheting projectiles continued until his magazine was exhausted and he sat down in the debris and cried. "Quiet," snapped another, who wore epaulets of yellow cloth on his shoulders. "Stand up."

"But they killed Soleni," the crying one spat. "Valenti said none of us would get hurt, and they killed him anyway. They're going to kill *all* of us!"

"Valenti said none of us would get hurt if we carried this off with precision. Obviously we were sloppy, and that's why Soleni's dead. Now stand up or you're going to be next." He pointed his weapon at the soldier who was still mostly a boy. "I said stand up, Tempeste."

Slowly Tempeste stood, and as he did so a voice called out from the shadows opposite Bullseye's resting place. "Go ahead and cry, you little bawl-baby. That'll make things a whole lot better, let me tell you." Madman cackled, more maniacally than usual. "There ain't never been a problem what couldn't be solved if you cried about it for a while. Just ask any woman." The soldier with the yellow epaulets turned, eyes wary, and followed the voice into the shadows. I read the name Tavagne stitched onto his chest. "Yeah, that's right. I said 'woman.' I just called you a woman, you sweaty-handed little—"

I heard a decisive burst of fire, and Madman fell silent. Tavagne reemerged from the shadows. I was panic-stricken, with my three comrades dead or certainly out of commission, and as I lay on the ground trying not to breathe I could not recall where I had heard that name Tavagne. He walked past me, toward the loading apron, but the third soldier, the one with the display unit, called him back before he reached it. "Benolo," he said with some agitation, and I strained my eyes until I could see why. "Come over here."

Benolo Tavagne joined the others near the bench where Maximo had so recently given up the ghost. Tempeste shivered and wiped his eyes. They stood over the old man's body, which had been knocked to the ground by the blast. It was torn and bruised, and a thin pool of blood had seeped listlessly from the wounds. "A civilian," said Tavagne wearily. "We killed a civilian. That's just great. How the hell did we manage this, Gannett, huh? You said there were only four people in here."

With the hand that held the display, Gannett motioned helplessly. "That's what the scanner said. Only four life-readings. I just—"

Tavagne turned his back and walked away. I could hear more gunfire and angry voices in the streets outside, and a few of the holomonitors droned on like psychotic village gossips. "Now what are people going to say about the Revolution?" said Tavagne with dangerous control. "That we're butchers of old men, that's what! I just hope no one else had a squad as incompetent as mine, because if they did we're all dead men." I turned my head unobtrusively and watched as he approached the lone black crate I had left sitting on the apron. He knelt beside it and fiddled with the fittings at its end. "In fact, I'm sorry it was Soleni who got killed and not one of you two grunts."

I heard the hiss of escaping air, and the lid of the crate swung up like an opening casket. Tavagne reached inside. Miranda Maria Montego, who should have been bound for space station *Tyrol* on the *Charon's Ferry*, sat up from within, her pale, thin hand clasped in his. Her hair was dull and lifeless. She looked about with wide eyes, wide pupils; she trembled, coughed, and put her arms around Tavagne's shoulders. "I thought you weren't going to come for me, Ben," she said, pressing her lips softly against his neck. "I thought I was going to die in there. I thought I'd be crushed under all the debris."

He stroked her hair. "Shh. I told you you'd be fine. The structural supports are stronger here under the hangar doors than anywhere else."

Had old Maximo risen from the dead at that moment, I could not have been more surprised than I already was. We tend to make compartments of our worlds, and Miranda had entered a compartment occupied by those who yet live but whom we will never see again. As the exchange continued, though, I realized that, with all my study of human phenomena, I should have expected exactly such a device from that terrible, lovely creature. All the clues had been laid before me, and I should have been able to guess what weight it had been that had dragged the floating crate off its balance. I realized then that I had never truly grasped the principles of psychology at all. *[Shots are fired far away.]* Wild stabs in the dark were all I had made, and that knowledge pierced me deeply.

Tavagne helped her out of the crate, and again they embraced, with the quiet desperation young lovers seem to find so fashionable. "How did things go with your grandpa?" he said gently.

She expelled a quick puff of air from her lips. "Same as always. He wasn't about to listen to a thing I had to say, and he was so wrapped up in his own little dreamworld that he didn't even..." She wiped her eyes roughly with the back of her hand. "He didn't even tell me goodbye. To him it was just 'get on that shuttle and get out of my life.'" She pulled away and looked into his eyes. "Freedom fighting's all I know that's ever impressed him, Ben, and I just want to do something to make him proud of me for once."

"I know," said Tavagne, drawing her back to him.

"As proud of me as I am of him."

"He will be. Once he sees this Revolution succeed, he'll be as proud of you as he's ever been of anything in his life."

One of the strange traits human beings possess is their willingness to be reassured by shamefaced lies. Miranda could not have believed what her young friend had just said, but obvious it was that she took comfort from it. They remained in their embrace for several more moments, until Benolo Tavagne released her and reached into one of his voluminous side pockets. From it he drew a shiny black sidearm, which he gave to Miranda. "Do you know how to use one of these?"

She took it from him brusquely. "Of course I do."

"Good, because you may need it tonight. Our orders are to secure the spaceport—no people get in, no ships get to land—and that'll probably mean scaring some folks off. Or worse." He took her hand and began to lead her back toward his two comrades. "It's going to be a long night."

Suddenly she stopped. Tavagne tugged at her hand, but she

would not move. Her back was as rigid as a flagpole, and the expression she wore was like that of a child viewing a horrorshow through a thick pane of glasticene. "Grandpa," she said through her confusion, in a voice like the uncomprehending chirp of a small bird as it tries to nudge its fallen mate back to life. Tavagne dropped her hand, his own face a mirror of her shock. He took a step backward, away from her. No one spoke, or even moved; it was as if the very air had frozen around them.

A mellifluous voice poured into the stillness, from historic Carvello Hall in Santaglio, Meridia, the voice of Pol Heyekassel, a man unpopular enough on his home world to be permanently exiled to this backwater planet in the name of foreign policy. "I'm sorry for that interruption, ladies and gentlemen, but it seems that there are yet elements on this great world of Tau Ceti IV who oppose the forward march of peace and progress. I have just been informed that a so-called 'Revolution' is underway in the westerly province of Belatria, one which has taken the lives of numerous of our transitional forces. In the dawning of this new age, there is no room for such irresponsible aggression, which is why a crack strike force is, even as I speak, departing from space station *Raldo*, bound for Calpurnia, the capital city of Belatria. This will be a regrettable but necessary demonstration of just how much tolerance the Conglomerate has for armed insurrection—"

Miranda broke free of her trance then, and, as she rushed to her grandfather's side to cradle his old gray head in her arms, I understood that every one of us in that shattered room was a fool, and that every one of us had been betrayed. *[Coughing, and sharp inhalations.]* That was our common heritage, our birthright, the bond that made us all members of a single vast and lonely species. It was not our social mores or our codependencies or even the pattern of our genes that made us one; it was our simple vulnerability, and the pride that brought it on. Pride is its own glass, its own trumpet, its own chronicle, and we that were proud had eaten ourselves up.

Tavagne approached his grieving lover and, in an attempt at mute sympathy, laid a hand on her shoulder. She shrugged it away. When he persisted, offering banal apologies, she stood and marched away from him without speaking a word. She was making her way toward the gap in the wall where the gate had once stood. Her stride was long and strong and firm and determined, but her face in the dimness was that of an old woman. To see such a transformation in the daughter of the woman of my dreams was almost more than I could bear. Determining that there should be no more betrayals to further darken that already dark night, and distilled almost to jelly with the act of fear, I pronounced her name aloud through my puffed and bleeding lips:

"Miranda."

She stopped as surely as if I had cast a chain about her neck. For the second and last time our eyes met, and hers were startlingly bright in that ageless young-old face. From women's eyes this doctrine I derive: they sparkle still the right Promethean fire; they are the books, the arts, the academes, that show, contain, and nourish all the world; and in them lies more peril than in twenty deadly swords. I wanted to run, to hide, to turn away, but I knew, or thought I knew, what last words old Maximo had wished to say to his granddaughter. To hold them back would have been the last unforgivable betrayal of that entire black evening.

I licked my lips, and, with all the emotion I could muster, spoke the magic words: "I love you."

If you have tears, prepare to shed them now, for this next was the most unkindest cut of all—or, if you like, it was the opposite, for sometimes we must be cruel only to be kind. With a countenance more in anger than in sorrow, she drew and raised her handgun, and I felt the ticklish kiss of its laser-spot as it danced on my face. Her hair blazed a sudden and vengeful red as she fired. The first burst struck my visor and shattered the opaque glasticene, but her pattern tightened on the second, third, and fourth shots, with results I have already described. Three hits, three very palpable hits, as ineradicable as the mark of the fingers that touch another person's heart. They do not love that do not show their love.

For several moments she stared blankly at her handiwork, and had I desired I believe I might have raised my rifle and returned the dubious courtesy she had done me. But at sundry times we must be kind only to be cruel, and so I left her to heaven and to those thorns that someday in her bosom would lodge, to prick and sting her with the vicious barbs of memory. When she understood what she had done, she threw down the gun and fled, across the stony cairn, through the gaping gateway, and into the throat of the night.

The revolutionary soldiers then fled as well, fearing the reprisals that were to come, comprehending nothing of what had transpired, and I was left alone with my pain and with the cold companionship of my thoughts. What first sprang to mind was the cryptic tale of the old golfer and his wife, and as I replayed that story in my mind, trying to figure out with which of the characters I most strongly identified, a strangely responsive chord rang out inside of me, and, so help me, I started to laugh. Echoes of that alien sound drifted back to me from the far corners of the spaceport, sounding so absurd that I could not help but laugh some more. I laughed and I laughed, until the hangar was so alive with the merry acoustics that I no longer seemed to be alone—until the pain of it all had me coughing up blood and wrenching my broken bones.

Here I have lain ever since, stabbed with a white wench's black eye, pinned and immobile, wounded and bleeding, dying and very much alive. How long I have been so I no longer know, though it can be no later than the early morning hours. *[The echo of a low, sighing wind.]* The strike force will arrive soon, and the medics with their nanomeds and preservatives and hermetic vacuum jars, to determine whether I need be mended. My fondest prayer is that I will not be here to greet them. Throw physic to the dogs: I'll none of it. *[Heartbeat and respiration slowing, slowing.]* O, amiable, lovely death! The country of my dreams lies just beyond my grasp, and there, amidst the hills whose heads touch heaven, awaits my one true love, the stuff of fancy made flesh, where *[cough]* fortune brings in some boats that are not steered.

What was it Hamlet said as ... as he drew ... his dying ... brea—
[The rest is silence.]

WHERE THEIR WORM DIETH NOT

1H.

LENNY DID EXACTLY AS HE WAS TOLD. HE USED HIS KEY TO GET them into the lab. He strapped them into the capsule and hooked up the biofeedback monitors. He programmed the travel coordinates into the onboard computer. Lastly, he exited the capsule and keyed the launch sequence into the control console.

The hatch sealed itself shut, and the capsule faded away into nothingness. Pastor Jacob Moody and his wife Gisele were off on their second trip outside the known universe.

Lenny cried and prayed they would never come back.

2A.

A FAINT SHIMMERING, LIKE A RISING WAVE OF HEAT, OBSCURES the verdant chaos of the jungle, where only a moment ago nothing stirred but a few restless animals and a cool evening breeze. A squawking cluster of bright blue life bursts into the air with the intensity of an exploding skyrocket, and the beating of a hundred sets of wings greets the bone-clean object that materializes on the jungle floor. It stands twice the height of a man and resembles an upended teacup. In the wake of the departing flock, the jungle waits expectantly, as if a giant hand will right the cup to signal the start of some strange and grand banquet. The back ends of three unlucky birds, spooked into flight in the wrong direction, protrude from the smooth surface of the capsule where their paths intersected its materialization. Just below them, the legend SIDETRIPS, INC. is printed in sharp black sans serif lettering, followed by a much smaller URBANA, ILLINOIS, U.S.A.

A gentle susurrus caresses the air, building from silence, as creatures of both the day and the night rouse themselves in the no-man's-land of evening. Something new has arrived in the jungle, unannounced. After several moments, the soft hiss of escaping gas cuts through the rustles and whispers, and silence reigns once more. A thin rectangular outline has appeared in the surface of the capsule; with stately grace, a hatch folds out and down on pneumatic hinges, to become a ramp extending from the open portal to the ground. Night creatures chatter in agitation.

The soft glow of instrumentation panels diffuses the darkness inside the capsule. A man's face appears suddenly above the lower lip of the hatchway. His thick, dark hair is tousled, as if from sleep, and he shakes his head to clear the disorientation as he peers out. His eyes abruptly narrow, going from cloudy to the cold blue of arctic ice. He climbs up and out through the hatchway to survey the scene around him with tightly controlled purpose. He is dressed for hiking, in tough jeans and a long-sleeved cotton shirt. A breath of wind stirs his hair as he pivots slowly on the ramp. Nothing else in the jungle moves.

He turns back to the hatchway, catching sight of the three trapped and lifeless birds. The already taut skin of his face seems to stretch even more tightly over his gaunt cheekbones. He leans into the capsule and calls gently, with a love that softens his demeanor, "Gisele? We're here, honey."

The background noise quietly resumes, like an exhalation from the jungle. He goes down on one knee, extends a hand into the half-light of the capsule. A woman with tangled wheaten hair, dressed similarly to him, emerges into the damp, cool air of the close of a humid day. She shivers, hazel eyes wide with wonder and fear—but those eyes are focused somewhere other than the here and now. He squeezes her hand, a gesture more for his own benefit than for hers, and leads her down the ramp.

The trees tower overhead like twisted columns supporting a thick green canopy. The light of the sun filters thinly to the jungle floor, falls in ragged, scattered patches. The man and the woman stop at the base of the ramp, and a patch of light strikes her face. He studies her with sharp concern, relaxing a bit when her eyes focus and meet his. This gaze is a well-worn conduit between them, and she tries to smile. The patch of sun slides away.

He cups his hand to the back of her neck, and with the ball of his thumb he caresses the long thin bruise that runs from the base of her ear, down the side of her neck, and disappears beneath her shirt. Loathing wells in his throat, and the unseen animals seem to withdraw in horrified sympathy.

This is the trail, the spoor, left by one of the six black worms that burrow relentlessly through her body, the worms they have come here to destroy. Two have lodged in her legs, two in her arms, one near her heart, and this one, the leader, not far from her brain. His throat spasms, and he fights the urge to push her away. Instead, he puts his arms around her, and after a moment's resistance they draw together like two magnets settling into a comfortable equilibrium.

The air is still, but charged with a reverent anxiety that reminds him of his congregation in the moments just before a sermon. Time for him to take the pulpit and lead out. But it is she, not he, who breaks the silence. "We shouldn't have come back here, Jacob," she says into the solidity of his shoulder. And her doubt claws at him with vicious black talons.

1G.

THE NIGHT WAS PICTURESQUE, A SCENE CURRIER AND IVES would have been pleased to feature on their January calendar had they lived in the right century. The snow fell in huge, lazy flakes, like apple blossoms drifting on the breeze. It stuck like frosting to roofs and window panes up and down the street, magically transforming the sleek prefab homes into gingerbread houses and fairy-tale cottages. It smothered the ground like a furry white blanket in need of smoothing.

Jacob noticed none of this as he marched up the walk to Lenny's front door. The weight in his coat pocket drew his concentration from the romantic nip in the air to its own evil chill. It's just for persuasion, he reminded himself. Just in case. Black centipede legs danced at the edge of his consciousness, leaving tracks in his mind as real as his own prints in the snow.

He stamped his feet on the front porch and looked back to the idling car where Gisele waited. His heart ached at her solemn beauty. He hated to leave her for even a few minutes, but the bittersweet taste of their love had become too much for him, and every bit of respite was not wanted but necessary. Besides, they had both agreed that this meeting should be handled by him alone, away from her and from the influence of the worms. He clenched his jaw and nursed the ache in his heart until it became a cold cinder. Then he pushed open the front door.

The house was oppressively warm and close. Jacob turned down the front hall toward the living room. Lenny, his childhood friend, sat in an overstuffed easy chair, feet stretched out toward the simulated crackle of his electric fireplace and back to the entryway. A small dish on the arm of his chair overflowed with crushed cigarette butts and powdery ash. A puff of smoke floated off like a departing spirit as Lenny lit another smoke. "Who the hell is it?" he said in a gravelly voice.

"We need to talk," said Jacob from the entryway.

"Oh, Pastor Moody, please enter my humble abode," said Lenny caustically. "My door is always open to a man of the cloth."

They had known each other for twenty years, ever since Lenny first moved to Urbana in the fifth grade, and never before had Jacob lost patience with him. This time, however, he strode darkly into the room, around the chair, and grabbed Lenny by the lapels of his bathrobe. He heaved him up and around and slammed him against the wall. "I'm not in the mood for any of your lip tonight. Is your family home?"

Lenny's face was pale and drawn, and his dishwater hair hung in unkempt strings. "They're, uh—Bev took the kids to their grandparents' for Sunday dinner. I've been a mess the last coupla days, and she doesn't want 'em around me."

"*You've* been a mess?"

His lower lip trembled. "Look, what do you want? I can't do anything for you, you know. It's all out of my hands."

Jacob glared at him coldly. "Haven't you learned to have more faith in yourself than that, Lenny? If not, you'd better learn fast, because tonight I'm calling in all the old debts. I saved your membership in this *parish*, I saved you from five years in *prison*, I saved you from getting thrown out of *college*—I even saved you from getting beat up your first day in school. What do I get in return? Two free tickets to a different universe, one where centipedes lay their eggs in people's *bodies*, for crying out loud, with the expectation of an endorsement for your company from the religious community. That's some deal, and I'm tired of it. It's your turn to be the savior for once around here."

"But I'm just a PR man, and they've pulled in a lot of big lawyers. What can I *do?*"

"I could care less about the lawyers. That's not the issue. My wife's *life* is the issue. There's a chance we can save it if you can send us back to where we went before. If you can do it tonight."

"That's crazy. What the hell for?"

"You don't need to know what the hell for. You just need to send us there."

"What makes you think I can run the equipment?"

Jacob leaned against him harder. "You *designed* their promotional demonstration. I *know* you can run the equipment."

Lenny squirmed like a worm under the knife. "We'll never be able to duplicate the exact coordinates. Every sidetrip is unique. No two parties end up in the same place."

"You sound like a commercial," said Jacob tightly, bouncing Lenny against the wall, "and you're just about as convincing. Those coordinates are on file somewhere. Your bosses didn't go into business just to send rich people out on nice little pleasure trips. They're sending them out as scouts for exploitable resources. That's where the money is. That's why everyone gets debriefed so intensely after a trip."

"Okay, okay. You're right." The corners of Lenny's mouth twitched as if he were trying to find guts enough to smile. "But what makes you think I'll help?"

"You won't do it out of Christian love and fellowship, that's for sure." Jacob put his face very close to Lenny's and spoke as softly as the falling snow. "You're going to help because, if you don't, your employers will learn about your suspended sentence for embezzling and your wife will find out who you've been sleeping with for the past two years."

The scant blood drained from Lenny's face. "That's a sacred trust, Jake. You can't do that."

"Things have changed." The clacking black feet were tiptoeing almost unnoticed through his mind. "You sent us to a time and a place where the old rules didn't apply, and you'll just have to live with what you brought back."

Lenny hardened his face. "Don't give me that. Your rules changed years ago, when you got married. All the talk you used to give me about how I could change my life if I just worked hard enough at it— I believed you and I did it, and then you turned around and handed the same thing to Gisele on a silver platter. She never worked for it." He took a deep breath and drew himself up as far as he could in Jacob's grasp. "You of all people should know divine punishment when you see it. You know what she was like in high school. She's never been anything but a whore."

With fists interlocked, Jacob swung and smashed Lenny across the jaw. Lenny landed on the floor like a thrown sack of grain, and Jacob pinned him there before he had a chance to get up. "You'll do exactly what you're told, or so help me you'll lose everything you've got that's worth anything."

Lenny whimpered and tears streamed down his cheeks. "They're already out to get me for using you on the promotion. They're blaming me for everything. If they catch me helping you, they'll crucify me."

Jacob's eyes glittered chitinously, like an insect's, as he forced Lenny's arm out straight on the floor. He pulled the gun from his pocket and jammed the barrel against Lenny's wrist, right in the hollow between the radius and the ulna. "Then you'd better get used to how it feels."

"Jacob!" Both men's heads whipped around to the entryway, where Gisele leaned against the wall like a cold and wet rag doll. Her voice was quiet, but nevertheless firm and commanding. "Stop it."

Breathing like a sprinter warming down after a heat, Jacob turned his attention slowly back to Lenny. His finger tightened on the trigger. Lenny's eyes were clenched shut in terror, and his back was arched. Jacob closed his own eyes, held his breath to the count of ten, and stood up. "Do you remember the harlot Rahab in the Old Testament? She and her family were the only ones spared in the destruction of Jericho, because she had mercy on the two Hebrew spies." He motioned with the gun. "Stand up. You're coming with us."

2B.

"THIS FEELS VERY, VERY WRONG, JACOB. LET'S GO BACK."

The man stops and leans wearily against the bole of a massive old tree, massages his temples. The sun has dipped below the treeline, sending forth wan, shallowly slanting beams of light that stretch out like arms straining through the bars of a cell. A patch of pale yellow flowers tremble in the slight breeze, as if torn between whether to watch the setting sun or the strange pair of newcomers who have wandered into view. Two small balls of fur perch delicately on a low branch, looking on with big sad eyes.

"What have we got back there?" he says, not looking up. "The doctors can't do a thing for you. The company's going to sue us for everything we've got, and Lenny'll probably have the police there waiting to arrest me for assault and battery when we get back. The ministry holds no answers for me anymore. At least here we have a chance, as slim as it is." He raises his head hopefully.

The woman has sat down in a patch of soft grass several feet away. They have not walked far, but she is weak with the fatigue of playing host to half a dozen voracious parasites. She picks up a broad, fluted leaf where it has fallen and begins to tear it into narrow strips. "We have no chance," she says simply.

"How can you say that?" He feels a stinging in his eyes, a tightness in his chest. "If we can just get to the Theater, we'll find a cure." He wants desperately to go to her, take her hand, comfort her, but he senses the time is wrong. "The answer's in those murals, I *know* it is."

"Forget the murals," she says, her voice rising suddenly. "How can we succeed after what you did to get us here? How can we expect God to help us after you used *blackmail* and *violence*"— she spits out the two nouns with distaste—"to force poor Lenny into helping us? You're supposed to be my example. What am I supposed to think when you act like that?"

His eyes narrow. "How much did you overhear there at Lenny's?"

Tears spill suddenly down her cheeks and she turns her head

away. "Enough," she says thickly. "Enough to know that nothing good is going to happen here."

"Gisele," he says helplessly, hands curling in front of him, "sometimes a lesser law has to be set aside if we're going to carry out a higher one. Weren't all the plagues in Egypt just blackmail to get the Israelites freed from slavery? The Lord ended up killing every firstborn male Egyptian before he got his way. I know it's not pleasant to think about, but I did what I did tonight because, to me, saving you is a higher law than anything else."

She turns her face back to him, but through her tears he seems to be swimming away. "Don't you think I know that? That's not what I'm talking about. I'm talking about what Lenny said about divine punishment."

Jacob shook his head. "You can't take that seriously. He didn't mean it. He was full of hate."

"I *wouldn't* have taken it seriously—if it wasn't what I've been feeling all day long." She draws her knees up to her chin and wraps her arms around her legs. "Jacob, I've tried to do everything right since I met you, I've tried to be a good person, but I just don't feel like God's ever forgiven me for the things I used to do. And seeing you tonight with that gun in your hand—" She buries her face in her knees. "I thought if I stayed in the car you'd be safe, but the bad influence on you just keeps getting stronger and stronger. You won't admit it, but I really *have* dragged you down to my level."

"That's not you talking," says the man, approaching her slowly. "You should know that by now."

"I don't know what's *them* thinking and what's *me* thinking anymore. It's like I've totally lost touch with myself."

With a conscious effort, he pushes away the writhing black specter that encroaches on his thoughts. Giving in is always so much easier, because it takes so little resistance. "Then they've got to go."

"I can't do it. I can't go any farther. I feel like the best thing I could do for you is to lie down right here and never get up again."

He bends down and picks her up in his arms. She is too light. "The sun's almost gone, Gisele. They said this jungle's supposed to be harmless, but that wouldn't be the first thing they were wrong about. We'd best be in the city before dark."

He kisses her before they set out, but it doesn't change anything. The two little balls of fur sigh and scamper off down the branch.

1F.

GISELE PACED RELENTLESSLY ACROSS THE LIVING ROOM, HUD-dled into a thick sweater and very pale. "Pastor Adams is a completely heartless monster."

Jacob watched her from the couch. The pacing made him nervous. Their house was well-appointed, but small, and he had always felt guilty for not being able to give her something bigger and better. The house of her dreams was a beautiful place—but unfortunately it lay in an alien city an unreachable universe away. "Honey, you shouldn't say things like that about him. He's one of my superiors ... and he's a good man. In his own way."

"I hate him. And you don't like him much, either." The low clouds in the west parted, and red light from the setting sun bathed the room through the picture window. "How can you work with that parish week after week and do so much good, then turn the pulpit over to a close-minded pig like him? He undoes in five minutes things you've worked months for."

The rent in the clouds healed; the room faded to gray. It looked like it might snow some more later in the evening. "I'm sorry. I just couldn't do it today. I couldn't face that congregation and tell them how to be happy and please God when I don't know how to do it myself anymore. Pastor Adams was very gracious to take over for me." He held out his hand. "Come here. Let me see how you're doing."

Hesitantly Gisele sat down at his feet. Jacob pulled her sweater down past her shoulders, then began to unbutton her blouse. "Why does he always have to harp on people like Potiphar's poor wife?" she said. "Everyone's always talking about what a vamp she was for trying to seduce Joseph. Well, maybe she needed affection and just didn't know the right way to get it. Maybe she was molested as a child and grew up with these sick, twisted ideas of what love and sex were all about. She was probably some pathetic little thing who desperately needed help, and no one would give it to her because all the pious hypocrites were too busy pointing fingers and trying to decide who would get to cast the first stone."

Jacob eased the neck of her blouse down over her left shoulder and examined the skin in the vicinity. The purplish line of discoloration had extended to the base of her neck. He closed his eyes wearily and buttoned her back up. Worm number one was that much closer to her brain. They had hatched in her ankle, and now three days had elapsed, three days of remorseless burrowing. How much time did that give them? A day? Half that? A few hours?

"Why are people like that?" she said unhappily.

"I honestly don't know."

She tossed her hair and looked up at him. "You're not comfortable with talk like that, are you."

"Gisele—"

"Be honest."

"Okay. No, not entirely, but—"

"That's what I thought." Her voice and manner grew distant. "Tell me, are you ever sorry you married me?"

"What kind of a question is that? No."

"Jacob, I want you to be totally honest. Are you ever sorry? Do I ever frighten you?"

Jacob felt a cold spot in his heart, as if an icy finger had reached in and touched him. "Sometimes I wonder if we're ever going to make it back to God, the two of us."

"'We' meaning me."

"No," he said firmly. "I worry about myself more than anything."

"What else do you worry about?"

He looked at the ceiling. "I worry sometimes that I'm not helping you progress as fast as you should be progressing."

Gisele bundled the sweater around herself tightly and seemed almost to withdraw into it. "I'll probably never progress that fast. What do you think about that?"

Jacob stared at the floor, not knowing what to say, trying to will the rapidly increasing distance between them to shrink. He was very frightened.

"I don't want to be there," she said, "but I often think that I'm standing a lot closer to hell than I am to heaven, and by clinging to you I'm dragging you down there with me. You don't need me. You need a woman who's more like you, up on your level."

He had to hunt to find his voice. "That wouldn't make me happy, Gisele."

She sighed. "I'm sorry for putting you through this. I'm not trying to drive you away—it's just that right now I have the blackest feeling in the world about our whole relationship."

"Me, too."

They sat in silence for several minutes, nearly touching but miles apart, each confronting for the first time the idea of a future without the other. Into that vast emptiness came a probing black tendril, and suddenly Jacob spoke.

"Gisele, it's not us. It's the worms. They're trying to drive a wedge between us. You're their host; they want to keep you, and they think I'm a threat to that." Wonder lit his face. "And if they're afraid of me, then there must be a way to fight them."

She looked at him with wide eyes. "How did you do that?"

"Do what?"

"You made the black feeling go away."

He put his arms around her and held her there for a long time. "It won't stay away forever," he said at length. "But as long as it's gone, I want you to know that you have more love and compassion inside of you than anyone I've ever known, and that alone makes me the most privileged man in the world. I'm never going to let you get away from me."

They separated and she smiled, but behind the smile was pain. "Thanks, Jacob. I hope that promise outlasts the next twenty-four hours."

"That's been much on my mind of late," said Jacob pensively. "I've been thinking, and since the doctors here can't do anything for you, the only alternative I can see is to go back to where all this started and try to look for some answers."

Outside, the sun had set and the snow was just starting to fall.

2C.

THE ABANDONED CITY SHINES LIKE A SCATTERED SET OF PEARLS in the late twilight. Scores of subtly illuminated alabaster buildings, Romanesque in design, dominate a scene of multi-leveled plazas, sparkling fountains, and staircases narrow and broad. The city is built on a series of low hills that rise gently from a wide jungle clearing, and its layout and architecture enhance rather than hide that fact. Not a single creature dwells here, and not one plant but those that were deliberately planned to be there. Its walls seem to await their mysteriously vanished inhabitants like a faithful wife awaits her sailor husband, with scrupulous care for her looks and arms open to none but him.

The city dwarfs the man who stands awe-struck at the jungle's verge, cradling his love in his arms. A broad plaza of flagstoned marble stretches away from them to a stairway and gate capable of admitting a whole legion of mounted cavaliers. Glowing crystal spheres flank the bottom and top of the stairs. The man sets the woman down on her feet at the edge of the plaza, and even through her depression and fatigue she is moved to whisper, "It's even more beautiful at night than it was during the day." A tear curtsies and falls from her eye. "It's like the stage for a fairy tale."

"But a Grimm one," the man says mirthlessly.

Together, hands linked, they walk. They cross the burnished plaza, footsteps clacking emptily, mount the sidelit stairs. They pass through the gate like lost toys wandering into a vast and exorbitant dollhouse display. Down parade-wide avenues and narrow, twisting alleyways, past moderate dwellings and monstrous edifices, up ramps and down stairs, the sweeping design of the city draws them in as inexorably as paper boats in a whirlpool. Drives them along, spurs them on, deeper and ever closer to its heart.

The woman's head turns as she spies the house of her dreams down a side street out the corner of her eye, but their pace carries them past too remorselessly to allow a detour. She tries to bury a sense of loss. That house is the only place she really wants to be in this big city.

The streets and structures possess an aloof beauty under the purple bruise of the sky, a sky that earlier blessed them with enough solar energy to light them through the night—but the man believes this city would glow of its own accord even without electricity. But still, there is something wrong here, a strangeness like the realization that a favorite book is missing from the shelf. He felt it before, exploring this city, but cannot put his finger on it.

"Jacob," says the woman suddenly, "there are no churches here."

That's it, that's what's missing. Marvel at the woman's perception and at this people's audacity collide in his mind. "I *knew* there was something missing," he says. "All these big, beautiful buildings, monuments to man's ingenuity and might, and not a thing to indicate tribute to *any* god. Not a temple, not a statue, not a spire, not even a lousy sacred emblem. It amazes me that an entire population could go through life without any expressions of faith."

She grips his hand tightly. "Maybe they couldn't. Maybe they ignored God for so long that he ignored them back—and they just vanished."

He nods. "Or maybe they didn't need him anymore," he says thoughtfully. "Maybe they outgrew him, found something better. Or maybe"—his brow creases deeply—"there was no worship here because there simply *is* no God in this particular universe."

A pall settles over the pair as tangibly as if they have been draped in a shroud. They continue along in silence, each lost and chilled in separate musings. Central to both their thoughts, though, is the idea that they may be here to perform an impossible task while hidden from the sight of God. Even this massive city seems suddenly dwarfed, thrown into sharp and insignificant relief, by the infinite empty reaches of the night sky.

"Or maybe," says the man with deliberate brightness, "this place is just one variation in a series of endless possibilities, and no people ever lived here at all. It just exists, always has, always will."

They curve past a building that might once have been a hotel or apartment building, and the ground slopes away sharply. Before them lies a deep depression, almost perfectly round and rimmed by cubic structures that, to scale, resemble children's blocks. Seven steep staircases lead down and into the wide bowl from various points equidistant around its circumference. Its depths are lost in shadow.

This is the center, the focus, the heart, of the city.

"If there were never any people here," says the woman, staring into the darkness below, "then there was never any cure here, either."

1E.

"THE ANSWERS TO ALL OF LIFE'S QUESTIONS," DECLARED PASTOR Adams with the authority of an angry parent, "lie here, in the Word, the Holy Writ, the Blessed Scriptures." He thumped his

Bible forcefully. "If we just learn from its lessons, and not just *learn*, but *believe* and *apply* and *live* by them, incorporate them into our very *souls*, then we can never—and I repeat, *never*—be led astray."

Jacob's hand lay on Gisele's thigh, idly massaging, and she covered it with her own. The were seated in the last pew of the modest community church, and every so often a curious or concerned parishioner would crane around and pretend not to be looking at them. Desiring simple anonymity, Jacob had forsaken his pastoral robes that day for a charcoal suit, but it was obvious that his appearance was causing a stir. Gisele regarded each onlooker stonily in turn, as if to confirm their secret suspicions of scandal.

Pastor Adams, especially, seemed never to let his eyes stray far from that back pew. The stained glass window behind him shone only dimly with the snowy light of afternoon. "Let me cite an example, my brothers and sisters," he continued, only slightly more subdued. "There are those among us who may be or may once have been afflicted by the temptations of lust and vulgar desire. Perhaps they went looking for it; perhaps it came looking for them. But when in that situation, however they got there, what can they *do?*"

His eyes narrowed harshly and he leaned low over the pulpit, hands planted to either side, as if daring the congregation to answer. "Joseph in Egypt faced that very question head-on. Sold into slavery by his jealous brothers, he ended up as chief servant to Potiphar, captain of the Pharaoh's guard. Potiphar was away frequently on business, and while he was gone his wicked, adulterous wife made frequent advances on the goodly Joseph. But Joseph never gave in. He just went on with his duties.

"Eventually, though, came a day when he could no longer

just ignore the unholy temptress. I quote from Genesis, Chapter Thirty-nine:

"And it came to pass about this time that Joseph went into the house to do his business; and there was none of the men of the house there within. And she caught him by his garment, saying, Lie with me."

The pastor's gaze crawled unrelentingly over the crowd, finally settling on Jacob. Gisele's hand tightened on his. "There he was, in the very clutches of temptation, face to face with the evil seductress. What did he do? Did he crumble? Did he give reign to his appetites? No. The Bible tells us: *He left his garment in her hand, and fled, and got him out."*

The eyes of the two pastors stayed locked for a long moment before the elder one returned to his scrutiny of the parish. Jacob's heart pounded irrationally, and his fingers dug into Gisele's thigh.

"There's the answer. When faced with sin, we don't *welcome* it, we don't *invite* it into our homes, we don't make pleasant *conversation* with it. We shut the door, we turn our backs, we *run*. We don't give it a fighting chance."

Pastor Adams straightened, towering over the pulpit. "But what if we *do* give in? What if the sin, the temptation, becomes so much a part of us or our household that we can't be rid of it without losing a part of ourselves? The Savior himself answered this question unequivocally in Chapter Nine of the Gospel of St. Mark:

"And if thy hand offend thee, cut it off: it is better for thee to enter into life maimed, than having two hands to go into hell, into the fire that never shall be quenched:

"Where their worm dieth not, and the fire is not quenched."

Gisele's muscles stiffened. Her hand left Jacob's and touched her breast.

"And if thy foot offend thee, cut it off: it is better for thee to enter halt into life, than having two feet to be cast into hell, into the fire that never shall be quenched:

"Where their worm dieth not, and the fire is not quenched."

Jacob felt a subtle wall going up around his wife. Her face was like ice, her jaw clenched. Her hand kneaded the soft skin to the left of her breastbone roughly, like a Lady Macbeth trying to rub out the damned spot—

"And if thine eye offend thee, pluck it out—"

—her eyes sparkled with unfreed tears—

"—it is better for thee to enter into the kingdom of God with one eye, than having two eyes to be cast into hell fire—"

—and she rose suddenly to her feet and slipped out the door.

Jacob delayed only one indecisive moment before following, and his footsteps echoed the black pitter-pat in his mind. The slamming church door bit off the next words of the sermon in the mid-phrase:

"—where their worm dieth—"

2D.

ON THEIR FIRST VISIT HERE, HE RATHER JOKINGLY DUBBED THIS place the Theater of Operations, and the name stuck, at least in his own mind. It seemed to deserve a name then, to beg one, but now he wonders if such a massive, impassive edifice might not be cheapened by the pithy titles and epithets applied by men. The Theater transcends any one name, any written or spoken definition. It simply *is.*

They descend a flight of stairs that begins steep and gradually flattens out the farther they progress. Every thirty feet or so down, they reach a landing, and, as they do so, lights automatically switch on in a ring level with them around the circumference of the wide amphitheater. Bit by bit, the bowl is lit as they continue down, revealing complex, brightly painted murals that cover the walls and draw the eye away from the shadowy reaches below. The murals depict scenes from city life, broad vistas of nature, families at work and at play, individual people in their individual pursuits, all interspersed seemingly at random, and all done in such a distant, camera's-eye style that the only emotion they convey is one of collective awe. It is the only visible art in the whole city, but it is not art the way the two visitors understand it; it is visual reportage.

Every so often the murals are interrupted by recessed alcoves, evidently reached by descent from the blockhouses above, from which onlookers would have a line-of-sight view of the floor of the Theater. A good percentage of the city's inhabitants could probably have found seating in them.

Ten landings down, the woman stops, flushed and wheezing. There are perhaps half as many more levels to go. She leans against the man for support, and he holds her tenderly. As she buries her face in his shoulder, too exhausted even to sit down, his eyes are on the vast display surrounding them. "You know the beautiful thing about these paintings, Gisele?" he says softly. "There are no moral judgments in them, no depiction of right or wrong, or good versus evil. These are the exact things you'd see if you took a walk through the city or the jungle, and there's no bias in the way they're presented."

He closes his eyes and rubs his cheek against her hair, which sticks to his stubbly whiskers like Velcro. "Maybe there are no churches here," he continues after a long pause, "because their religion was a completely internal thing. No outward show, no hypocrisy, no judging—only a set of common beliefs that in the end came down to just hashing things out between yourself and God. Maybe there's no one here because they were all taken to heaven, like Enoch or Ezekiel."

A moist warmth kisses his shoulder, and he draws back to see the woman's tears flowing freely. The long, thin bruise now extends to her temple. Her tears are not tears of relief at his speculations, or even bittersweet tears. They are the overflow of stoically borne pain.

Heart and throat constricted, he supports her weight as they continue their descent into shadow.

1D.

"This had better be good to get me up on a Saturday," snarled Covington from the video screen. His hair was matted from sleep and his features as harsh as a whetstone.

Mitchell turned to Jacob and Gisele with an exasperated, apologetic expression and drummed his fingers on his desktop. His clients, his friends, sat holding hands on the sturdy but threadbare couch, the only other major piece of furniture in his office. Jacob had obviously not slept much in the past two nights, and Gisele had only done so under the influence of heavy sedatives. They were shadows of their usual selves. He returned his attention to the screen. "You promised you'd have a counterproposal out to us by five o'clock last night. We never got it."

"We underestimated the time it would take," said Covington, running a hand through his hair. "Settlements can *never* happen that fast. We're going to need at least a full week."

"My clients don't *have* a week, dammit! The situation is *bad.*"

"Well, if it's so bad, then what's the woman doing out of the hospital?"

Mitchell took a deep breath. "There's nothing the hospital can do for her, so we got her out this morning. Now, it *is* a long shot, but there's a neurosurgeon we can bring in who might be able to do her some good, *if* we get some compensation. Otherwise, she'll be dead or insane within a matter of days, and you'll have a massive lawsuit on your hands."

"Oh, really?" Covington scowled darkly. "Let me tell you a thing or two about contractual agreements, Mr. Mitchell. Your clients signed a contract with my clients that promises compensation for death or injuries sustained on a sidetrip *only* in the event that the rest of the items of the contract are adhered to strictly. In returning to this universe with six parasites in her body, Mrs. Moody has not only violated the clause which states that no alien organisms are to be brought back from a sidetrip, but she has also placed her fellow citizens in jeopardy if those worms ever decide to take up residence in someone else's body. We could not only countersue your clients for everything they own—we could have them legally quarantined and incarcerated." Mirthlessly he chuckled. "I don't see where you have a case."

Ashen-faced, Gisele drew close to Jacob, but at the same time he was rising to his feet. "Where are your ethics, man?" he demanded hoarsely, outrage creasing his face. "Where's your compassion?"

Covington's smiled was guileless and wicked. "There's no percentage anymore in ethics or compassion, son," he said with avuncular condescension. "This is the twenty-first century."

"Yeah, but only just barely," whispered Jacob.

The video screen clicked off.

Mitchell turned to him, downcast. "I'm sorry, Jake. I did my best."

"Don't be sorry for us. Be sorry for him." Jacob helped Gisele to her feet, feeling like a hypocrite for giving such advice.

2E.

AN ORNATE WHITE RAILING SURROUNDS THE LOWEST LEVEL OF the Theater of Operations, broken at seven points around its perimeter where the seven staircases impinge and descend. The man and woman continue down through the gap in the railing without a pause, for he is supporting most of her body weight and is powerless to do more than point their gathering momentum in the right direction. Delirium has seized the woman as the first worm nears the end of its relentless journey toward her brain, and she moans and mumbles half-sentences as the man struggles to keep her on her feet.

They touch the bare floor at the base of the stairs, and white light floods the small arena they have entered. It is perhaps a hundred feet in diameter with walls ten feet high, and a large marble slab lies in its center, waist-high. Heavy purple curtains sheath the walls in the gaps between the staircases, but the curtains begin to rise with the turning on of the lights, revealing a series of seven murals more stylized and symbolic than the ones on the sides of the bowl.

The murals are all very similar. Each one portrays a young woman lying on an altar or an operating table, and a young man poised over her with a knife at the ready. Black squiggles are painted at various points on the women's bodies—one on each extremity, one on the torso, and one on the face—evidently representing parasitical worms like those that afflict the one living woman in the arena. Each man and woman has a gray circle painted on his or her forehead, and a red one on his or her chest. Each couple's circles are joined by thin white lines, red to red and gray to gray.

Seven different women, seven different men. Do they represent seven specific historical couples, or do they stand for a whole cross-section of people, all required to pass through the same barbaric ritual? These musing's cloud the man's mind as he lays his loved one down on the slab. She thrashes weakly and tries to rise, but he pushes her down and murmurs gentle words of comfort. When she has relaxed sufficiently, he kisses her and turns to study the murals more closely. "The answer's here somewhere," he says, half to himself.

The woman's eyes focus and she says, with the clarity of the onset of pain, "I love you, Jacob. No matter what happens here, I don't want you ever to forget that."

The bright lights suddenly dim to a third of their full intensity, and a black pedestal rises from the floor at the head of the slab. Atop the pedestal in a slight, shaped depression rests a sharp black shining scalpel.

The woman spasms and an unearthly scream tears loose from her throat. It is the shriek of a cyclone, with the intensity of a furnace and the depth of an ocean trench. A black stampede descends on the man's thoughts. The first worm is drilling into her skull.

He snatches the knife from the pedestal, holds it high like a maestro's baton. His impulse is to slash and rend, to tear the worm bodily from the woman's temple. But he drops the knife to the floor as he realizes that the fingers of the most skilled surgeon back home could not successfully accomplish what he is being forced by circumstance to attempt. He sinks to his knees, crushed by the weight of love, of despair, and of the piercing screams that mount higher and higher to fill the black expanse of the night.

1C.

JACOB JERKED SUDDENLY AWAKE AND ROSE TO HIS FEET WHEN the door to the operating room opened. His eyes were red and his hair in disarray. It was one o'clock on Friday morning, and the technicians and debriefers who had helped rush Gisele to the hospital when the capsule had reappeared had long since gone home to bed. "What's going on, Doctor? How is she?"

Dr. Bennett pulled off her left glove and snapped, "Keep your shirt on, son. She's still alive." Then she breathed deeply and massaged her cheekbones. "I'm sorry, Pastor. I'm a little on edge and we're both tired. Let's sit down."

She seated herself wearily in a cushioned chair. Her graying hair stuck out from its bun in tangled little wisps. Jacob sat down across from her and wiped his palms on his thighs. "I thought I heard screams earlier," he said, "but no one would tell me what was going on. Is she all right?"

Her lips compressed. "She's in stable condition. That's about the most encouraging thing I can tell you right now."

"Why? What's wrong?"

"The creature you say stung your wife didn't poison her like we thought at first. It laid its eggs in her—and they hatched very quickly."

Jacob looked at her blankly. "Laid its eggs?"

"Yes, and now there are six small worms living in her lower leg."

"Living...? You mean you didn't take them out?"

"Pastor—" She shook her head and grimaced. "We tried to remove them, but we couldn't."

"You—couldn't...?" He trailed off, not wanting to understand, not trying.

"Those organisms are like nothing that exists here on our earth," she said. "This may be difficult to believe—it's difficult for *me* to believe—but apparently they can influence the thoughts and feelings of their host and, to a more limited extent, other people nearby."

"So what does that mean?"

"It means that when we made our initial incision in your wife's leg and tried to remove one of those worms, her vital signs went crazy and she started screaming like one of the damned. All we can speculate is that these things have developed some kind of psychic bond with your wife. When one was threatened, it channeled intense pain right past the anesthetic and into her brain until we left it alone." She regarded him levelly. "Those were the screams you heard."

"Well," said Jacob, struggling for words, "what makes you think it's something psychic? Why couldn't it be, say, neural?"

Dr. Bennett closed her eyes. "I thought it was neural at first, too—all of us did—until we all started getting very irritable. And not just irritable, but harsh, on edge. We were snapping at each other. My surgical team is just not like that. I don't know how to describe it, but it was like we could all *feel* something alien prowling at the edges of our minds." She snorted grimly. "That must sound pretty crazy, right?"

"Yes, it does. And while you're here talking crazy, what happens to my wife? Are you just going to leave her like that, all full of parasites?"

She stood. "It's my professional judgment that we can't re-move the parasites from her body without killing her, or at the very least inducing significant mental trauma. Meanwhile, they seem to be burrowing their way up through her leg, and it's my guess that they're heading towards her brain. I couldn't venture to say what'll happen when they get there, but I'm sure it won't be pretty."

Jacob shot to his feet. "And you're just going to sit back and watch it happen?"

"There's nothing else we can *do*," she said with wearing pa-tience.

"I don't believe you." Synapses were firing in his brain, pieces of the puzzle falling into place. "Back where all this started, they used to do operations like this on people all the time with noth-ing more than a knife. You have a lot more resources than that, so don't tell me there's nothing you can do."

"How do you know what they used to do?"

"I saw it in a painting."

"Well, that's good enough for me," she said testily. "I know a good neurosurgeon we can bring in from Chicago if you like, but he'll just tell you the same thing I've told you, and your in-surance probably won't cover the additional cost."

"Thanks, that's very helpful," Jacob muttered.

"It's the best I can do." She turned to walk away, thought dif-ferently, and turned back. "If you have so much faith in this dead race of yours, Pastor, then maybe you should have stayed there and let *them* treat your wife."

"Maybe I should," he said to her retreating back. Choking on his sorrow, he sat down and closed his eyes. In the morning he would call his lawyer and together they could weigh his options.

2F.

SCREAMS. SHRIEKS. BLOODCURDLING, HEARTRENDING CRIES OF horror and pain. The man rocks back and forth on the floor, buffeted by the horrific sounds, trying somehow to crawl inside himself, to escape the tortured aural onslaught. The screams from this woman whom he loves more than his own life pierce him to the very center, threaten to drive the sanity right out of his head to roost somewhere in the dank jungle. She is a part of him; how can he listen to her suffering and yet be helpless to stop it?

Black, undulating feet beat a hideous tattoo at the limits of his perception, echoing like footfalls in an empty church, telling him to run, run away. Joseph ran away from *his* bad situation, and aren't we supposed to follow the example sct forth in scripture? The thrashing black feet drove him up from his knees. Escape this. Get away, far away.

But there, right before his eyes, is the woman. Writhing, convulsing, back arched, eyes rolled back so only the stark whites show, lips peeled away from gleaming, feral teeth, bruised temple pulsing with the vicious hunger of a lowly worm— The feet say to run, but he knows that, however far he goes, that nightmare image will follow to haunt and harry his every step. His hands clench into quivering hooks that long to bury themselves in his own eyes, to stop the transmission of pictures to his brain. A black, segmented cavalry encircles his mind, marching like the ancient besiegers of Jericho, setting up sympathetic vibrations to smash down the walls of his will.

Unless we can find some way around that psychic link—

"There's no way around you black bastards!" he rages. "So come at me! Don't hang back! Come here and take me on! Throw it all at *me*, let *me* take it, and leave the woman *alone!*"

The black noose tightens, and the screams do not stop. They build and build into a cacophony fit to rattle the very foundations of space. They fill his ears like molten steel, plugging up the acid of rage, frustration, and impotence that eats huge holes in his soul. But it is not until he opens his eyes once more that he realizes that the screams are no longer hers. They are now his own.

She lies on the slab as comfortably as if she were sleeping in her own bed. Her eyes are closed, her breathing is regular, and a very faint smile touches the corners of her mouth. But discoloration still stains the side of her face like a splash of bright purple ink. The man falls to his knees and clutches his temples as if to crush them, for agony bites there with a thousand little drill bits for teeth. He feels every gnash, twist, and slash of the leader of the worms as if it were his own skull being penetrated. Tears streak his cheeks, but cannot cool the fire beneath; knuckles press fiercely into the sides of his head, but, of course, the worms are not there.

Clenching all the muscles of his face, he claws the floor until his fingers stumble across the fallen black scalpel. It is cool to the touch, and there is a certain solid reassurance in its obsidian finish. Shakily he stands, the rending of his head threatening to press him back down to his knees. He steadies himself with a hand against the slab and sets the knife against the woman's temple.

Countless centipede legs flail suddenly against his hand, and he drops the knife reflexively. It clatters against the slab and skitters to the floor. The cold touch of chitin lingers in his hand. He consciously slows his breathing and eyes the knife through a haze of pain. It lies still—hard and sharp, black and unmoving, completely unlike the worm he was *sure* for a moment had been thrashing in his grasp. It taunts him with its immobility.

His head is like a buoyant, burning balloon, resisting descent as he drops gingerly to his knees. Even the slight impact of the floor jarring his bones drives a hot spike through his consciousness, and tears seep like blood from the wound. He snatches up the scalpel and rises quickly. His head lolls to the right as if pushed off balance by the horrendous drilling. He leans against the slab once more and readies the knife.

When the illusion hits again, he is prepared. He keeps his eyes fixed firmly on the knife, and, though he can *feel* a living worm twisting in his grip, his sense of sight tells him it is not so. The knife is still a knife. Cautiously, trying not to compensate for the illusory motion in his hand, he presses the tip into the skin of the woman's temple.

Five black tendrils of thought sail past the man's mind, one from the first worm to each of its cohorts. Wild grinding pain erupts in his thighs, upper arms, and chest. His legs nearly buckle, and his arm jerks away from the woman. The pain subsides to dull, localized throbs. He buries his face in his hands, the smooth blade of the knife cool against his forehead. This worm, he realizes, is the dominant of the six, due perhaps to its proximity to the woman's brain. Attack it first, and the others go crazy, maybe causing enough internal hemorrhaging to kill her. The five subordinate links will need to be excised first.

As he reaches for the woman's leg he sees red on his left hand. He stares at it blankly, then touches his temple. A thin trickle of blood snakes away from a shallow gash, the sting of which is lost in the broader wash of pain inside his head. A similar laceration marks the woman's temple where his knife jerked away, but its edges are clotted and no blood has escaped.

Pulse throbbing mercilessly in his ears, he climbs onto the slab, kneeling and straddling his wife's legs. He knows he will not be able to complete the operation standing up. Her face is peaceful and calm, oblivious even, as he slashes open the leg of her pants. He touches the soft skin of her inner thigh. A long, thin bruise, like a roadmap from nowhere to nowhere, demarcates the flesh halfway from knee to crotch. "I love you, Gisele," he whispers as blood and tears drip from his face. "I always will."

He places the tip of the knife on the bruise, and he cuts.

Agony stabs his own thigh and rips apart the flesh with burning fingers. Fire dances in the wound, and spots dance before his eyes. The incision under the knife opens cleanly, bleeding just enough to clot properly—but an angry red stain appears on the man's pant leg and grows until the fabric is saturated. Droplets of blood spatter on the woman's pants and speckle the pristine marble. He bites down on his tongue to keep from passing out. The worm is not visible so he cuts again, deeper, until the knifetip clicks against a hard, segmented body.

He shifts all his weight to his good leg, whimpering through clenched teeth. His fingers slide into the incision and under the worm, and he tears it loose with a savage pull. The pain is like acid on a raw nerve. It eats at him, flails him, scourges him. To push it away, he focuses on the worm.

It resembles a black centipede and is about as big as his little finger. Bits of tissue cling to its dozens of barbed legs like bait on fishhooks. He scoops the knifetip through its underbelly and lays it open, then severs the beady head. He flings the inert husk aside and starts on the other leg.

His vision is awash with red, his nervous system shrieking like a banshee, as he removes the second worm. He lays atop the woman's body to remove the third and fourth worms from her upper arms, for his legs will no longer support him, even kneeling. His arms are sheathed in wet, crimson gloves and rasp-edged nails seem to transfix his biceps as he raises himself to attack the fifth worm. He slices into the satin skin above her left breast to pry the thing out from between her ribs. His heart feels ready to rupture, like a bladder stretched to the breaking point and filled with molten lead.

He eviscerates the worm and tosses it alongside its fallen comrades. His arms will barely move, and loss of blood has weakened him nearly to the point of unconsciousness. Prone atop her body, he turns her head to the side and makes an incision in her temple.

As the knife touches the leader of the worms, a black psychic tether leaps from her mind to lasso his. Her thoughts open up to him like a blooming flower, and he is hit by an unchecked barrage of distrust and hatred. Straight from her to him.

1B.

THE EARLY AFTERNOON SUN SHONE STRONGLY INTO THE OPEN bowl of the amphitheater. "I wonder what this means?" said Jacob, studying the seven murals with open curiosity. "What went on here? Some kind of human sacrifice?"

"No, nothing like that," said Gisele from the center of the arena. "This place is too civilized." She hopped up and sat on the edge of the marble slab. "Looks more to me like surgery or bloodletting or something."

"But in an amphitheater where half the city could watch?"

"Maybe the city was full of medical students."

Jacob chuckled. "Then I guess we could call this place a Theater of Operations."

Gisele smiled and laid back on the slab, hands behind her head. She closed her eyes. The sun felt warm on her face. "Thanks for bringing me here, Jacob," she said. "I know you didn't really want to come, and it was mainly a favor for Lenny, but I feel better here than I have for a long time back at home."

Jacob turned from the murals and approached the slab. "How so?"

"Our world is such a hard place to live in. There's no black and white anymore, just a lot of shades of gray. There's evil everywhere, and no matter how good you try to be, you can't get completely away from it." She rolled onto her side as Jacob sat down beside her. "I would have run off a long time ago and become a hermit if it would have solved anything. The world has too much of a hold on me, and I can't stand it. I hate it, in fact."

He ran his fingers through her hair, and she asked, "Am I the kind of wife you want me to be?"

He thought. "Not always," he said. "You're the kind I need and the kind I love, but you don't always match up to what I think I want. If you did—if you had to live up to all my crazy expectations—you wouldn't be the same person and I probably wouldn't love you. If you change with time then that's great, but I'd never force you into being someone you're not."

She smiled and reached up to stroke his hair. He closed his eyes. When he opened them, she was gazing at him warmly. He felt a tug at his heart, and he bent down and kissed her.

Gisele gasped suddenly and pulled away, her face creased with pain. "What's wrong?" said Jacob.

She drew a sharp breath. "My ankle..."

He turned his head. A black centipede had mounted the slab. It was a foot long, with a tail like a scorpion's, and its stinger was buried in Gisele's ankle, just above the leather of her shoe. Jacob grabbed the creature, wrenching its stinger from his wife's flesh, and flung it across the arena. It bounced on impact, righted itself, then skittered down a small hole in the floor.

Jacob tore off Gisele's shoe and sock. Her ankle was already beginning to swell, and they had been supplied with no first-aid kit. "This does not look good," he said tightly. "I think we need a doctor."

2G.

HE DIGS THE WORM OUT OF THE INCISION WITH SLIPPERY FIN-gers and stares it in the face. It wriggles in his grasp, flailing its legs and clacking its spiky mandibles. Blood streams down his cheek, but the pain from his temple is nothing compared to the river of hate flowing into his mind. It is sobering, like being thrown into an icy lake.

Resentment, frustration, guilt, hostility, it all streams across in a foul mixture, and it is all directed at him. He scans his mind desperately for a glimpse of the black presence that has become so familiar, but it is not to be found. Terrified, he realizes that this is the woman's subconscious, laid open as cleanly as if with a scalpel, and it is bleeding.

He sees himself through her eyes—with loathing and disgust at his hypocrisy, disbelief and anger at his self-righteousness, helplessness and rage at his non-acceptance of her. But it's not true! he screams at the roiling river, but its inexorable flow turns his words back against him. It *is* true. You *are* all those things.

The worm's beady eyes glitter conspiratorially. The man's mind goes entirely blank, and he gropes like a blind man for a hold on who he is, where he is, why he is there. Then the river comes crashing back to flood him with renewed comprehension. For a moment he had been totally lost, in darkness, and—

The worm! It can not only *influence* thoughts and feelings—it can *erase* them!

Excitedly, he sets the worm back down on the woman's temple, reaching past the pain and the hurt to summon up all the love he has in his heart. It rises like a fine mist. The worm will erase all the hatred from the woman's mind, and he will release the mist to distill like dew on her pristine subconscious. She will know him exactly as he is, she will love him, and she will at last be the person he wants her to be.

The worm noses into the incision, a yellowish fluid dripping from its mandibles. Clean white bone lies beneath its feet.

Exactly the person he wants her to be.

Exactly.

Pain strikes anew, like a power drill through the temple.

Sudden terror rises in him like lava gushing to the surface of the earth. He grabs the worm and squeezes it until yellow slime bursts from its underbelly and its body casing cracks.

"I can't make you someone you're not," he says, laying his cheek against hers. His bitter tears rinse tracks of blood from both his cheeks and hers. "Even if that person hates me."

He loses his grip on consciousness, and the crushed husk of the worm drops from his fingers.

1A.

THEY HAD ONLY BEEN IN THE CITY FOR TEN MINUTES WHEN Gisele stopped and put her hands to her mouth. "Jacob," she said thickly, "it's my dreamhouse."

It stood three stories high, with pillars and gables and turrets and porches and balconies, all in sparkling white. She took him by the hand and they explored it for half an hour, and the delight on her face was like nothing he had ever seen.

When the novelty had worn off for him, though, he said, "Let's go see some of the rest of the city."

"But I want to stay here awhile longer."

"It's okay, honey. We can always come back."

2H.

HE AWAKES ENFOLDED IN SOFT WHITE SHEETS, IN THE BEDROOM of the house of her dreams. She watches him from across the room in a formfit recliner, knees drawn up to her chest, smiling contentedly. "Those are some wicked lacerations," she says. "You'll probably have scars for the rest of your life."

"You're here," he croaks in surprise. "*I'm* here."

"Of course you are. I couldn't leave you half-dead back in the Theater, could I?"

He tries to sit up, but his body is too weak and too sore. He sinks back into bed. But you hate me, he protests silently.

—*No, Jacob, I love you.*

Her voice startles him and his eyes widen. She smiles slyly. Her lips had not moved.

—*You only saw what the worm wanted you to see*, she says. —*It filtered out the other ninety-nine percent.*

"But—"

—*Shh. Don't talk. Just let me show you what got left out.*

He closes his eyes and relaxes, and she is all around him, in every breath of air, every beat of his heart, every spark of life in his soul. She loves him, actively, from across the room.

—*What happened back there, Gisele?* he says after a long, long, beautiful time. —*What did it do to us?*

She strokes his heart gently. —*It gave us our citizenship. This is our city now. This is our house.*

—*But we can't stay here. Not forever, anyway.*

—*No, not forever*, she agrees. —*Not even the original inhabitants could stay here forever. They had to get out and expand their theater of operations. We'll have to, too, eventually. But not yet.*

They stay where they are for the rest of the afternoon, exploring the mysteries of each other's souls.

BITS OF A GRASSHOPPER

1.

IN HIS MIND'S EYE, DANIEL SAW HIMSELF TEARING HIS WIFE REbekah limb from limb.

No, he told himself firmly. That must not happen. That *will* not happen. He clawed sweat roughly from his face as he crashed through the weeds and wild grass that had encroached on his property like a besieging army. The weeds, cracked and drying in the early afternoon sun, rose nearly to his chest. They seemed to clutch at him, to scourge him, as he passed, but Daniel barely noticed them.

He was saving Rebekah's life. He could *not* allow himself to hurt her.

He crossed a narrow trail worn down through the weeds by the animals from the surrounding hills who foraged each night in his garden. He spared the trail only a cursory glance. If he'd wanted, he could have set sonic traps to keep the animals away, but he didn't mind sharing with them. He and Rebekah would survive the drought easily enough, as would their chickens and cow, because the hygrolysis unit he had erected in the north field culled sufficient water from the air for them to get by on. The wild animals, however, were not so fortunate. For a moment Daniel could see the bodies of deer and coyotes in his mind, of chipmunks and skunks, porcupines and rabbits, starved to death and rotting, their carcasses bloated in the heat—

But this image stayed with him for only a split-second. His mind was already far ahead of his body, anticipating the release he would find in the barn.

His passage sent swarms of clicking grasshoppers into the air, insects with bodies the size of his ring finger, startled from hiding by the rude force of his stride. They flitted away in all directions with the lightness of butterflies, gaily displaying colorful wings they could only show off when in flight—some of dusty yellow, others of sapphire blue, or of blood red or forest green, or the beautiful rare ones of soft velvet black. Another time Daniel might have chased these old nemeses of his with a stick to gather bait for fishing—but scant days before, the stream had slowed to a trickle and vanished. All that remained of its treasure of rainbow trout were stinking, pale husks shaped like fish but colored more like maggots.

With or without fish to catch, however, this was no time for clubbing grasshoppers. Daniel's need was stronger than even the fierce, unblinking eye of the sun. His blood felt as if it were boiling.

Only Allyce would be able cool it for him.

Like projectiles shattering his spine, he could feel Rebekah's furious eyes against his back. She was watching him from the kitchen window of their log cabin. Daniel's sixth sense told him this, and he did not think to doubt it, despite the fact that Rebekah's agoraphobia was so extreme that she wouldn't let him to depolarize the windows even in the black of a moonless night. This was not the first time he had felt her eyes follow him from that window after one of his nasty blow-ups.

Her angry, familiar words still rang in his ears—how she hated living on the surface, hated their isolation, hated their proximity to so much that was untamed, wild, and alive—how she hated carrying a baby in her *stomach*, for God's sake, when it would take just a quick trip down the canyon to get the thing removed and hooked up to an incubator. "Oh, come on, Rebekah," Daniel had said with patient exasperation. "Natural childbirth has been the method of choice for ten thousand years."

"Can you stop being flippant for just half a minute?" shouted Rebekah in a voice tinged with hysteria. "You don't have *any* idea what's happening to me. I'm cooped up in a tiny *wooden* house that seems about to collapse every time the wind blows, and I have a *parasite* in my guts, feeding off my own *body*. I'm *lactating*, Daniel. Do you have any idea how *repulsive* that is?"

He pushed her gently down into her form-fit recliner, which molded itself to best support her lower back. The chair resembled a soft-shelled, dull-gray egg, and Rebekah's swollen belly protruded from her tunic like its smaller ovoid sibling. "You're pregnant," Daniel said. "You're *supposed* to be lactating. You have to feed the baby when it comes." He had just turned thirty, and to him fatherhood was the most exciting prospect of his life.

"When it comes? When it *comes?* I've got news for you, Daniel. The baby's already *here!*" She pointed to her bulging stomach. "It's *been* here for seven months!" Little muscles in her face began to tremble. "If I have to stay in this house any longer with this *thing* inside me, I'm going to go out of my *skull!*"

"You need to try spending some time outside. You'll feel better if you do. I *know* you will. You just don't know what you're missing. Flowers and trees and insects and birds..."

"*Organic* things—*that's* what I'm missing!" She shuddered. "There's nothing but rot and disease and decay out there! Millions of little germs and viruses floating around!"

"Not millions," Daniel said with a wry smile. "Billions—trillions, even."

"Daniel—"

"I go outside every day, and have we come down with any disease?"

"That's not the *point!* This is an *obsession* with you, wanting to be outside all the time! I can't *stay* here, Daniel! I need to get back to a Project! I need to get this thing out of my stomach! I need some *freedom!*"

"Freedom? You want *freedom?*" Daniel's lips curled away from his teeth in an involuntary snarl as his secret heart began to beat inside of him, all flippancy peeling away. The hateful technological conveniences Rebekah demanded—protein synthesizer, ultrasonic shower, waste pulverizer, air sterilizer, holographic art, all the banal miracles of science that hid the reality of the planed-log walls from his eyes and his nose and his fingers—all seemed to press in on him as if he were trapped in a shrinking silicon room. He felt a primal scream erupt from his second soul. His face became twisted, and his voice was like the bellow of a grizzly bear. "All the freedom you could ever want is right outside that door, and you won't even crack a shutter to *look* at it! You sit in here feeding off the tit of science like some little infant rat whose eyes haven't even opened yet! Here, take the starter to the car! Drive to Salt Lake and get yourself a cozy little room in the Catacombs where you can live like the *maggot* you apparently want to be!"

Wide-eyed, Rebekah shrank into the recliner, plainly aching to snatch the starter from Daniel's outstretched hand, but too frightened to move. Tears collected in the corners of her eyes like little expanding beads.

"Come on," he said softly, but with clear menace. "The car's a mere twenty meters away. Go ahead." He paused, watching her, as the ancient transfigurative flame raced through his veins.

She didn't move.

"Huh," he grunted. "Can't even get up the courage to walk twenty meters through a little grass."

He turned away, shaking his head and returning the starter to his pocket. But suddenly he hurled the object at the wall and spun back to her. "What do you know about freedom, anyway? What do you even know about being cooped up? I spent four *years* floating around the asteroids in a little tin can. I know what being cooped up is all about. I've *earned* my freedom. I wouldn't trade it for anything. I *give* you yours, and you spit it back in my face."

The beast inside him was manifest in his face—he could tell from his reflection in Rebekah's terrified eyes. He didn't try to hide it or hold it back. He only turned on his heel and stalked out of the house before his curling, self-willed hands could do something to her that he would never be able to live with afterward.

The blazing sun was like a hammer, and the crawling sensation would not leave Daniel's back. At least she was looking out the window. At least he'd gotten through to her *that* much. He still felt her fear, but what his sixth sense couldn't tell him was what was going through her frightened mind. That was the one thing he'd never known, even in the months when they'd had a semblance of happiness—what was going on inside her head.

And that was something he would probably never know.

His animal self wondered why that bothered him so much.

Daniel broke out of the tall grass and onto the dusty verge before the old tumbledown barn, half a dozen chickens squawking and flocking around him in hopes of a handful of feed. The wood of the barn was warped, cracked, and brittle, the planks weathered to a dark, tangy gray. A host of grasshoppers settled to the ground away from the chickens, blending in perfectly with the soft yellow dust, little clouds of which rose and collapsed which each of Daniel's steps. The hot, stale darkness inside the barn called to him, and his bloodstream burned hotter the nearer he approached.

Daniel knew he was an anachronism, an artifact plucked from its proper place in the past and cast up among the artificial ruins of the present—like this ancient barn, but from a time even more remote. His was the soul of a savage, trapped in the body of a modern man. Years before, in the Miami Project, when the first realization of his dual nature had awakened in him, he had been unable to cope with the disparity. The two young women who lay dead and dismembered in a stagnant sewer near the mouth of a Project service tunnel could attest to that. In his panic after the killings, he had fled into space with the Merchant Marines, but soon found that the irresistible magnetism of Mother Earth was even more intense from a hundred million miles away than it was from the heart of that overcrowded Florida rats' warren which ten million people called home. Now Daniels made his home in the countryside of northern Utah, a place where his elemental nature lay appeased enough to slumber quietly inside him.

Most of the time.

And for the times when it was stirred snarling to life ... there was Allyce. That was the one precious gift the asteroid belt had given him—Allyce. She had followed him home from the barren, rocky wastes of spaces—would follow him *anywhere*, he had discovered—and she awaited him here, in the hot, stuffy dark, always ready, always able, to ease his raging fever.

He pushed open the door to the barn, and its hollow, timeless creaking sent the grasshoppers winging away in a flurry of clicks and extravagant colors. The dead air reached out like a fist, seized him as he entered the sweltering dimness. He pulled shut the door behind him. Fingers of pallid, grainy light knifed through the slats in the wall, cutting the ground into yellow strips, like a negative of the bars of a jail cell.

By rights, this place should have housed the cow, but the tottering structure was no longer any fit abode for a proud farm animal like Crusoe. The cow now shared a field with the hated gunmetal-blue hygrolysis unit.

Allyce, however, who had no pride to insult, seemed to be very happy here.

The ladder to the rickety loft ascended between two decaying support beams. Daniel started toward it, but was immediately assaulted by a harsh, synthesized parody of his own voice, slicing through the stale air like a manifestation from a parallel universe. "That's far enough, you pathetic degenerate!" cried the voice. "Where on God's green earth do you think *you're* going?"

The Sentinel. *Damn* that machine!

Daniel spun around, face contorted and shoulders hunched as if to strangle the very shadows clustered around him. "You shut up!" he yelled, his fever flaring. "You just shut *up!*"

"I knew you couldn't do it, Danny boy," said the voice of the Sentinel with an electronic sneer. "Twenty-three days under your belt, and you just couldn't hold out any longer. What a waste, what a—"

"I said *shut up*, you fool machine!" A weathered length of timber lay in the dirt and dry straw at Daniel's feet. He snatched it up with both hands and brandished the old wood like a baseball bat, sending dust motes into a swirling dance through the grainy bars of sunlight. "Shut up and *leave me be!*"

"What a miserable waste, Daniel. Two more days and you would have set a record. *Two days* is all. Any *real* man could held out—but then, you're not really a man at all, are you? No, men don't run away from their problems the way you do. They don't take their anger out on someone else. They have more self-respect than that. They're mature enough to talk things out."

Daniel advanced on a corner of the barn where the shadows seemed to gather most thickly. "Keep it up," he said, waving the timber. "Just keep it up."

"Or what?" taunted the Sentinel. "You gonna smash me to little bits with that great big stick of yours? Knock the walls in on me? Or you gonna do me like you do poor Allyce every time, with just your bare hands? Oh, you're a man, all right, Danny boy, yes sir. So go ahead and prove it. Beat a helpless machine to death. Go on! *Do it!*" The voice sank to a menacing, staticky hiss. "Or are you afraid to?"

Deep in the shadows, barely visible, a speaker grille and a bit of machinery protruded from the matted straw. "You can't talk to me like that!" said Daniel, his voice like a sudden windstorm, rising from a whisper to a scream. He cocked the timber and sprang, swinging.

Sadly, the voice said, "You disgust me."

A sudden burst of white light filled the barn, and a sharp black shadow flashed briefly to life on the far wall. Daniel screamed, the length of timber flying from his hands. He hit the straw, rolled, clutched his thigh. The timber crashed harmlessly against one wall, raising a cloud of dust when it clattered to the ground. "My leg!" Daniel cried. "You almost took off my *leg!*" His teeth were clenched in pain. "What are you trying to do, *kill* me?"

"Oh, please," said the Sentinel. "It's just a little burn. Don't be such a baby. The beam wasn't even at half intensity." Then it added slyly, "You thought you managed to *break* that laser last time, didn't you?"

Daniel said nothing, containing his rage and humiliation only with great effort. A Sentinel was a form of ANI—artificial near-intelligence—designed to serve as a psychological watchdog. It could be custom-programmed to perform nearly any sort of therapy imaginable. Daniel, however, had configured this unit not to act as a private therapist, but as a verbal torturer, sparing no mercy in its attacks on his pride. He had done this as a measure of self-denial and self-protection—to try to keep himself away from Allyce.

In a practical sense, then, he had brought this assault upon himself. The Sentinel was, after all, only an imperfect reconstruction of the loathing he felt for himself in the wake of his encounters with Allyce—often for days afterward.

Daniel staggered to his feet, bits of straw and dirt clinging parasitically to his back, and limped in silence to the ladder. Weak sunlight streamed through the chinks in the walls like sour, ineffectual lymph. The dust motes hung nearly motionless, tiny particles suspended in a rank solution. To Daniel, the world felt dry and close, slow-baked into stasis. With anger dancing in his fingertips and heat behind his eyes, he turned and regarded the Sentinel buried in the corner. His mouth twitched.

Then he very deliberately turned his back and began to ascend the ladder.

"Twenty-three days of perfect self-control, Daniel," said the machine softly, in a voice hollow with regret. "Twenty-three days. Think about what you're throwing away."

Daniel paused briefly on the rungs, feeling as exposed as a fly on a freshly scrubbed wall. The dust particles in the beams of light were like a belt of tiny asteroids. His knuckles whitened. "You don't *even* understand," he said, and the words nearly caught in his throat.

Resignation filled the Sentinel's voice. "You were doing so well."

Daniel ignored the comment and climbed.

The air was hotter in the loft and more stifling than at ground level, and the atmosphere, perversely, was much gloomier. The swelter was like a dank, knotted tarp, ready to smother and suffocate any intruder. As Daniel hauled himself up through the trapdoor, the planking creaked and squealed dangerously, like the warning moans of a lost, wounded spirit, but he knew from long experience that the old timber was more than strong enough to support his weight. Back in the old days, they'd known how to build things to last—from wood, not from metal. Despite its appearance, the barn was quite sturdy, and its members could take a great deal of punishment.

This he also knew from long experience.

A curious, ticklish emptiness crept into Daniel's stomach, exciting him in a vague way. His testicles had retracted, and despite the heat he stood shivering as he waited for his eyes to adjust to the dim light. The instincts of a savage flowed through his veins; he stood perfectly still, knees slightly bent, hands loose at his sides, nostrils flared and testing the air. The barn muttered and groaned to itself. A trickle of cold sweat ran from his armpit down his side, sending chills across half his body like an army of tiny swarming insects, but still he did not move. He waited, and the hollowness in his stomach grew.

This was where Allyce, who had followed him invisibly across so many millions of kilometers, now chose to meet him when his need demanded it.

After several moments of silent stillness, a faint luminosity began to develop in the gloom. It could almost have been a phantom, a trick of the dim light, no brighter than the radium dial of a watch in a shuttered room. But the glow took slow shape before his eyes, resolving into soft contours and surfaces, like a figure languidly surfacing from moonlit waters. Breasts coalesced first from the thin incandescence, like hot gases collapsing to form two stars—tipped with ember-bright aureoles that flared briefly and dimmed as they cooled. The slope of a chest emerged, smooth and white as a snowfield. From the rounded, delicate shoulders which appeared next extended arms as strong and shimmeringly translucent as those of a marble statue, and the clean lines of a neck rose like a tower to where the head and features were still being born.

The emptiness was a raging pit in Daniel's stomach. His loins now throbbed with a painful intensity, and he felt as if fluids from all throughout his body were being sucked down into that roiling cauldron. Spots swam before his eyes; his hands and knees trembled with an inexplicable chill so deep that his muscles might have sheathed bones of ice. He held himself perfectly still, but his eyes hardened and his body tensed.

"Daniel, I am weak," the apparition said, a hiss through lips shifting like mist. Her shape blurred, drifted in and out of focus. "I am, perhaps, too full of you at last. I have warned you before."

Some distant, rational part of his brain registered alarm at this announcement, but to Daniel it was like hearing the evening news through a locked door. His mind was awash with animal imperatives that drowned out all other considerations.

He did not see a woman before him; he saw a mere set of visual tokens targeted to his lusts, and in those tokens lay satiation. He growled her reservations aside. "*Now*, Allyce."

She nodded wearily and her eyes closed.

His patience thinned and frayed as he waiting through her instantiation. It had never taken so long before. This frustrated him, but he held the emotions inside, nurtured them into tools that he could use for cleansing, for purging, for striking back at the world. First one part of her, then another, rippled in and out of existence with the taunting power of images glimpsed through a peepshow window. She writhed, gently, abstractedly at first, but with increasing ardor. Soft yet vital pastels coruscated through her body, and her dance was like that of a mad snake trying to wriggle back into some long-shed skin. Anger and longing seethed inside of Daniel with acidic vigor, seeking release, burning apertures through which to spurt. The pressure built and built, pounding like the sea against a retaining wall, until it seemed he must explode—and *still* it built—and *still*—

—until suddenly she solidified, with a great gasp like that of a newborn taking its first breath. Her face was hard, embittered, and spiteful, but filled with an almost mocking helplessness. Her skin was white as an eggshell, taut as a wind-stretched sail. "Feed me, Daniel," she said. "Fill me with your anger."

Daniel's breath caught in his throat, and a shudder raced through his body. For an instant he was frozen, poised at the crest of an immense crashing wave, fighting for air—and then he was upon her, hands knotted in her hair, teeth sinking into her throat, nails raking her shoulders and breasts.

Velvet-winged grasshoppers scattered like bursting shells, clicking in alarm as they dispersed.

WHEN HE WAS SIX, DANIEL HAD BROUGHT BACK A GRASSHOPPER from an illicit excursion outside the Miami Project. The memory still stung like a lover's rebuke.

Even at that age, he was dissatisfied with his life underground, although he could never have articulated his longing for the feel of wind and sunlight on his face, the coolness of long, springy grass beneath his feet. The fiftieth anniversary of the nationwide relocation into underground Projects had already been celebrated by the time Daniel was born, and extensive renovations completed by his fifth birthday. He had never experienced the out-of-doors, and he had no clue how tiny and restrictive his own environment was in comparison to the world of the surface.

The Projects were a panacea to the fears of environmental catastrophe harbored by the lower and middle classes. Space habitats had existed for decades—and the struggling Martian colonies were well on their way to permanence—but these were not even remote options for those not blessed with wealth. The government-subsidized Projects were seen as a haven from crime, pollution, and every ecological paranoia imaginable. By the time of the Golden Jubilee, far more people in America lived below ground than above.

Renovations during the sixth decade of habitation had been sweeping, but not all-encompassing. The Projects were so huge, the needs of their swelling populations so pressing, that small matters like sealing off unused intake ducts had been overlooked. Once he had found his way from the bright, strip-lit corridors of the upper residential levels into the forbidden surface access tunnels, the restless and enterprising young Daniel had only to punch through a few rotting air filters and wriggle up a hundred yards of piping to at last emerge into the sunlight for which he had yearned so long without realizing it.

He felt as if he had found his way back to a home from which he had long been banished.

The landscape he explored was not a hospitable one, however. He emerged onto a city sidewalk from the rusted enclosure that housed the air intake duct. There was sunlight and wind aplenty, but the only grass he could see grew not in wide rolling fields, but in unchecked riot through large cracks in the asphalt streets and in the alleys between abandoned tenement houses. Exotic birds wheeled and screeched over the remains of the city in great flocks, but seemed disinclined to settle to any perch. Young Daniel prowled the city like a lonely predator, searching for something he did not understand, but which he felt he had lost. Angry hurt gnawed at his stomach as he realized that the surface world was nothing like the one they portrayed in his lessons at school. Where could he find the vast fields of vegetables and grain he had learned about, tended by robot laborers and only a handful of human overseers? Where could he find the great tumbling rivers, and the massive hydroelectric plants that tamed them? Where could he find all the animals from his picture books—not birds, but the animals that were earthbound like himself, earthbound and still free?

As the sun trickled like a bright tear down the western sky, the young boy sat on the fractured front step of a brown-brick apartment house, clusters of corrosive-resistant hypodermic needles glittering near his feet, and cried.

And that was when he noticed his first insect.

It was a tiny black ant, crawling up his ankle, tickling like a droplet of sweat. The boy pinched it delicately between his thumb and forefinger, plucked it from his leg, and watched in utter delight as it struggled through the fine hairs on his arm like a microscopic explorer penetrating deepest jungle growth.

He felt a strange kinship with the little ant, and when he discovered whole columns of them marching in perfect order across the cracked concrete, he realized that his focus had been much too wide on this first outing. There was a whole new world at his feet, just waiting to be explored and conquered.

Black ants, red ants, flying ants, ladybugs, striped beetles, scurrying roaches, caterpillars, centipedes, termites, silverfish, fat black spiders spinning gauzy webs—he became emperor of them all, herding them here and there like tiny sheep, tossing them into the air and watching them fly away, pitting them one against the other in gladiatorial combat. Daniel was in ecstasy, and he scarcely noticed the skinned knees and elbows that came from scraping along the sidewalk in an attempt to see the world from a bug's perspective.

But soon the shadows lengthened, the alleys grew dark and chill, and it was time to leave his new friends and troop antlike back to his own underground colony.

Near the mouth of the intake duct, however, he spied a new kind of insect, what he would later learn was a common green grasshopper. A strange desire seized him, and almost before he had thought about it the spindle-legged insect was trapped between his cupped hands, and Daniel was wriggling back into the Project with his prize.

But as he threaded his way through the evening strollers back to his parents' apartment, young Daniel found that his captive had spit slimy brown juice into his palms. He was repulsed and angered by this. In this fit of childish rage, he tore legs and wings from the helpless creature and flung the bits to the floor—then immediately fell to his knees, tears streaming down his face as he tried to put the creature back together, sobbing, crying, "I'm sorry, I'm sorry," over and over, as a throng of curious onlookers gathered in the harsh white light of the corridor, and little Daniel couldn't see a thing through his tears until his hysterical mother fought through the crowd and dragged him back home by his collar and gave him the soundest beating of his life.

"I'M SORRY, I'M SORRY, DON'T HURT ME PLEASE I'M SORRY," Daniel cried as he rocked back and forth on his knees, hugging himself tightly as if to keep his body from falling to pieces on the planked floor of the loft. Tears coursed down the runnels of his cheeks, and sobs racked his frame. He couldn't understand why what he had done was so wrong. He had never actually been *forbidden* to go topside—it was just that people rarely did. Unspoken fears about what lay above ground, however unjustified, were pervasive beneath the surface, those few who ventured out were regarded with suspicion, forced to undergo involuntary decontamination before being readmitted. But these were not things that a six-year-old could readily comprehend.

The blistering sunburn that lasted all week was more than enough punishment for little Daniel. Even the memory of his awful session in the decontamination chamber could not match his horrid guilt at having dismembered his helpless grasshopper friend. The grasshopper had not died quickly. Its wide black eyes betrayed no expression, but its thrashing antennae had told the whole story. It had been as if the insect were struggling to flail itself to death in its agony. Only one of its hind legs remained, and its feeble attempts to hop away nearly broke Daniel's heart. No matter how he tried, he had not been able to reattach the dismembered legs—and he found he lacked the courage put the grasshopper's suffering to an end.

"I'm sorry," Daniel cried again, weakly, and he buried his

face in his hands. But his hands were streaked with something slimy and cold, something from which he recoiled as if it had burned him. He stared at his hands in horror, at the thick black ooze that stained them, then slowly turned his head. He knew what he would see—knew that he did not want to see it—but he couldn't help himself. His hands, frozen, mocked him.

Allyce lay all around him on the floor of the loft, in a dozen or more pieces, all of them leaking black ichor. He had been especially thorough today. Ice trembled in his stomach and loins; the wet patch in his trousers felt like melting snow. Thankfully, Allyce's head faced away from him so he could not see her eyes, but the other parts seemed to pulse in the dim light with some kind of bloody vitality. Her left hand, severed raggedly somewhere above the wrist—by his own teeth, he could tell from the imprints—shuddered mightily and rolled over onto its palm. Its fingers flexed, and like a wounded scorpion it began to drag itself across the floor, leaving a trail like thick black ink.

Daniel stood and slowly backed toward the ladder. He felt as if that hand were crawling up the back of his neck. His knees were like gelatin, and his heart screamed and hammered inside of him. He watched in dread fascination as the self-willed hand butted up against a large fragment of arm, feeling this way and that for the place where it once had connected.

Daniel cast a guilty glance over his shoulder as he began descending the ladder, as if some accusing witness might await him at ground level, and his foot slipped and missed a rung. He caught himself before he could fall, but his impact against the ladder rang out like a shot. Allyce's head rolled over on the floor of the loft, and her eyes opened nearly level with his. Beneath a torn and matted scalp, those eyes were filled with compassion.

A bubble formed on her lips as she tried to speak.

Daniel clung to ladder with his eyes squeezed shut, and he stayed there sobbing until the urge to vomit had passed.

2.

TWENTY-THREE DAYS. AS HE TOILED UNDER THE ANVIL OF THE sun, the words cycled through Daniel's head like a mantra, endlessly spinning, endlessly dancing, like water spiraling down some infinite basin. Twenty-three days ... twenty-three days ... think about what you're throwing away....

Days had passed, days and days—how many he was no longer sure. Maybe a week, maybe more. All he knew for certain was that it was nowhere close to twenty-three. The Sentinel could have given him a precise count if he had cared to ask, right down to the minutes and seconds, but Daniel refused to go any closer to the old barn than was absolutely necessary, not even to feed the chickens. If the stupid birds were hungry, they could come after their feed themselves. He could not go there. The barn was a symbol of his weakness, his cowardice, his betrayal...

Rebekah! he cried silently. How am I capable of doing this to you, time and time again? He stood stiff and straight as a pine tree in the middle of his garden, weeds of a sickly, virulent green clenched in each fist, eyes closed and face to the sun. He loved her. He loved her so dearly that it was worse than an ache—it was a *cavity* around his heart. She was the mother of his child, in a more complete sense than any female parent he had ever known, including his own. A piece of him and a piece of her, inseparably fused, nurtured and warmed in her belly. The thought of it awed him. He loved Rebekah so much that, when she failed to return or even to acknowledge his love, or when she disparaged the little miracle she carried inside her, a helpless passion welled up in him, and the voice of a beast snarled from the back of his brain. He wanted to shake her until she understood what he needed from her, until she was willing to give it.

Tears like sparkling diamonds left trails in the dust on his face, and the weeds he crushed in his hands bled milky juice that dripped to the ground like spilt semen. They had spoken very little in the past several days. Daniel could only guess at and invent horrible reasons for Rebekah's silence, but as for his own, the shaky, tenuous self-respect that had taken him twenty-three days to build up had been obliterated in a quarter of an hour by an act he hoped never to repeat, one that left him incapable of any meaningful exchange with the woman he loved. That first night—how many days ago?—Rebekah had come to him, had pressed his head to her swollen belly, had touched him, caressed him, done all she could for him in her pregnant state. It was a mute, tender gesture of conciliation after their argument, but Daniel refused to be consoled. The very same stirrings of desire she awakened in him had betrayed him once that day already. He had been unable to return her gesture.

The sun beat down, and suddenly Allyce's specter arose in his mind, taking shape from the dense mists of thought, interrupting his grief. Her breasts, light as clouds, seemed to defy the lordship of gravity; her hair floated and beckoned like underwater moss in a corona about her face. Traitorous desires stirred in his loins, intensified.

Daniel fell to his knees amidst the carrots and potatoes, teeth clenched, fingers knotting in his hair. It wasn't fair. He did not want to be aroused. He did not want to face the choices arousal demanded of him. He wanted to banish Allyce forever from his life and his memory. He wanted to root up his manhood in a spray of blood and burn it with the other weeds, or bury it, or fling it away—anything, so long as it could never again betray him. It was the seat of his animal consciousness. Without it he would be much better off.

The simple way out.

But at that he shook his head, violently, as if to dislodge some demon from its perch above his ear. That was not the simple way. The way he had always done things, letting the beast rage free— *that* was the simple way. The simplest way *possible*, in fact. It required no effort, only a surrender of the will.

The other way, emasculating himself, would be tough—very tough. It was tough even to *think* about.

There *were* other options. And, Daniel thought, if he had grit enough even to consider castration seriously—then maybe he had grit enough to actually go *through* with one of his other tough options.

He jumped to his feet, feeling a sudden new lightness, as if layers of heavily caked filth had fallen away from his skin. He reached the cabin in a few moments, pushed open the door and stepped through the slight pressure differential designed to prevent airborne viruses from getting indoors. Daniel knew the air curtain was completely unnecessary, but it made his wife feel more secure. "Rebekah?" he said timidly. He peeked around a corner of the entry hall and into the pine-and-silicon living room. "Are you here, honey?"

"I'm here," she said with little enthusiasm. She sat watching the holovision tank from her big egg-shaped recliner. He could just see the back of her head poking up over it. "Where else would I be?"

"I don't know. It's just something to say." He moved to the recliner, a peculiar sensation twisting around in his stomach—but one not unpleasant. Leaning over from behind, he put his hands on her shoulders, kissed her gently on the top of her head. Her honey-blonde hair smelled of wildflowers, and Daniel smiled at the incongruity. She would never *consider* putting a real flower in her hair, not one that might be contaminated with microbes bearing some dread disease, but she didn't think twice about wearing the *aroma* of flowers. He kneaded her shoulders, which were as tense as cables, and kissed her again. Her back arched slightly and sigh of contentment escaped her, but she did not look at him. He could still sense a kind of apprehension about her.

He circled the chair, squatted on his heels between Rebekah and the holotank. He took both her hands. They had been folded over her abdomen, and they felt warm, like fresh bread. Her eyes shied away from his, but not before he glimpsed the small sparks of hope that she tried to hide from him. The sight of it was like a knife between his ribs. He squeezed her hands in what he hoped would be taken for reassurance. "I love you, Rebekah," he said, ducking his head almost shyly. "Sometimes I wish I didn't, because I know I only hurt you, but I really do. I love you."

She leaned her cheek against the top of his head, eyes pressed shut, and he accepted her touch gratefully. But after a moment he drew away from her. "I love you," Daniel said again, "and there's something I need to tell you."

IT WAS IN HIS FRESHMAN YEAR AT UNIVERSITY THAT HE TOOK another person with him to the surface for the first time, a girl. She, like Daniel, was planning to major in agricultural engineering. Unlike Daniel, however, she had never been topside. The prospect was an exciting one to her—or so she told him. If she planned to devote her life to the science of large-scale farming—

still very much an abstract goal to her—then she allowed that she had better find out soon whether or not she could bear a life in the wide-open spaces, beneath the infinite sky.

As for Daniel, he had been making regular trips out for over a dozen years. The beatings had never stopped him, nor even discouraged him, but now that he had an apartment of his own—due in large part to the generous scholarship he had earned—he enjoyed a much greater freedom in his comings and goings. This meant a greater isolation, however, for in the intervening years paranoia in the Projects had increased to such a panic level that even the most vital shipments of food were delayed for up to a week while they underwent decontamination procedures. Few people trusted an individual who spent the majority of his free time exterior to their closed, hypersterile environment.

But the girl was different—or so Daniel thought. They had met at a career-planning seminar, in a group discussion on the relative merits of surface employment, and in a matter of days they had become inseparable. They reveled in the rush of strange emotions, in the thrill of shared confidences. When they were together, they could not keep from touching; when they had to be apart, they sank into lassitude and melancholy. So when Daniel asked her to join him on one of his trips to the world aboveground, her answer was never in doubt—though the prospect of asking her sent a flutter of butterflies through his stomach.

They went out through an old, disused service tunnel that opened into what had once been a city park. They could have used one of the more conventional exits, but Daniel still found it convenient to slip in and out without attracting notice. He knew the system of access shafts like the back of his hand, and knew Miami proper almost as well. He rarely encountered another human being in his visits to the surface—when he did, he tried to stay carefully concealed—and so, in these hours free from watchful eyes, his animal self began to assert itself more and more, although he still did not recognize the disparity between the two halves of his personality. He would lose himself prowling the shadows of the silent streets, perhaps stalking some small bird or animal, creeping as close as he could without startling it away, pouncing upon it—and on occasion making a modest meal of his prey. In these instances particularly, he felt it prudent not to reenter the Project through one of Security's authorized inspection points—not wearing blood-stained clothing. There was no sense in exposing himself to undue scrutiny.

Thick-boled trees and dense undergrowth had long since overrun the park, and Daniel and the girl emerged from the tunnel into a lush tropical oasis, crammed down between glowering ranks of old apartment buildings. A canopy of broad leaves screened out the sun overhead and trapped moisture and heat as if between glass walls. Daniel took the girl by the hand and led her out into the greenery, chattering with animation about what to her were incredibly strange sights and sounds. But within a dozen steps she had planted her feet, caught in the grips of sudden agoraphobia. When he tried to tug her along, she broke free and bolted back to the enclosure that shielded the entrance to the service tunnel. He lunged after her without a second thought, the animal in him already snarling to the fore of his brain.

He could not later say what instinct it was that had registered her desertion as a threat—only that that instinct had performed its task swiftly and brutally. He concealed the girl's torn body inside a thick patch of shrubbery, desperately, feeling the eyes of a thousand imagined observers upon him as he came out of his savage fugue. No one saw us leave, he tried to reassure himself.

No one knew we were going. Only a few people knew we were even *seeing* each other.

But these thoughts could not ease his panic. Project Security were a thorough and dogged lot, especially when it came to missing persons. The Projects had a reputation for freedom from most violent crime, and that reputation had to be protected. There would be a painstakingly meticulous inquiry, and if the body were to be discovered...

Daniel slipped back into the service tunnel, returning after half an hour or so with an old toolbox he had once seen lying around in the access system. Hungry magpies scattered away from the body at his approach. The hacksaw he had found in the toolbox was rusty, and its blade snapped more than once before his task was complete, but there were replacements. When he was finished, he used a small crowbar to pry the grate from a nearby sewer opening, and there the girl found her final resting place.

Daniel wiped sweat from his face with a bloody hand; it was steamy and humid under the trees, and the stagnant sewer air only contributed to the general miasma. He had always known he was different from everyone else, but he was only beginning to understand the real extent of those differences. The implications of it sank in slowly, as if realization were a steamroller running him over in no particular hurry. The more it worked on him, the more he knew he had to try harder to fit in underground, to make no waves—and the more convinced he became that he would not be able to do it.

When a second girl joined the first, after even less provocation, Daniel stopped trying at all. The tension and guilt were like bands of steel, squeezing the breath out of him. Inquiries were in process, and Daniel felt an irrational conviction that he would eventually be caught. It was time to get out for good.

The Merchant Marines became his ticket.

He underwent the requisite physical and psychological tests, and within a week received his posting as Ordinary Crewman to a freighter bound on a four-year tour of the asteroid belt. In truth, the psychological tests showed him to be only marginally fit for this duty, but crewmen for such voyages were in short supply, despite the excellent pay and benefits. The mining interests on Mars and in the asteroids were the lifeblood of the interplanetary shipping lines. If cutting corners was what it took to keep supplies moving out to the miners and ore moving back to Earth, then corners would be cut.

Away from Earth, Daniel's animal self lapsed into a kind of hibernation. The vastness of space soothed him and seemed to quiet his dangerous urges—at least initially. Daniel was reticent with his fellow sailors, but not disliked by them, and he soon worked his way up to the status of Able-Bodied Crewman, with a commensurate increase in pay.

But the farther Earth receded into the blackness at his back, the greater its pull on him became.

It happened so slowly that he did not notice it until well over a year into the voyage, but once he recognized it he realized that the sanctuary of space might be what finally destroyed him. On two occasions he lost patience with his shipmates, and the savage inside him nearly slipped its reins and went rampaging. The beast was growing stronger. Daniel feared that one more altercation would cause him to lose control. The asteroids were close at hand, but the freighter would spend a year among them, unloading supplies and taking on processed ores, and then it would be another eighteen months until he could be free of the ship's confines and once more run barefoot across the face of Earth.

He knew he would never survive that long.

But then the relic was discovered.

Almost precisely as the freighter was crossing the invisible boundary that marked the official limit of the asteroid belt, a mineralogist serving double-duty as junior navigator detected a large quantity of some unfamiliar titanium alloy embedded in the surface of one of the larger nearby objects. Laser spectroscopy revealed that the alloy was one never developed by man. The ship's course was altered, and Daniel found himself part of a hastily formed survey party. The primary tasks of this party were to have included gathering seismic data and drilling ore samples that the experts on Earth could use to determine the asteroid's potential as a mining site.

But as visual contact was established with the surface of the asteroid, it became apparent that this would be no ordinary survey mission.

An alien starship was imbedded there.

The survey crew, working in skin-tight oxygen-recirculation suits, soon determined that the starship's age was something on the order of fifty thousand years. A few of the more interesting devices they found were salvaged from the wreckage for further study; the remainder were left to future expeditions. The asteroid's position, mass, and angular momentum were charted, and the file on the alien ship was closed with this terse adjudgment: LIFELESS.

Only Daniel could appreciate the irony of this pronouncement—for as he, unaccompanied and in foul temper due to the comment of a thoughtless shipmate, fighting to restrain the beast within, and losing, had scouted out a relatively undamaged section of the ship's interior, a strangely pulsating fog had coalesced about him, ages-old impulses had coursed singing through his blood, and he had raged through his first encounter with the alien being called Allyce.

FOR THE FIRST TIME SINCE DANIEL HAD ENTERED THE ROOM, Rebekah dared to look at him—though hesitantly and indirectly—and dared allow the little flickers of hope to show in her eyes. She squeezed his wrists. "What? What is it?" she said, too vulnerably, too eager to be hurt again if it might bring them back together.

And Daniel experienced one of the few moments of perfect insight that he would ever know. He saw that the confession he was on the verge of making would end their marriage as quickly and finally as if one of them had been killed. He saw also that unless he were to reach out to her somehow, with something of real value to offer, then their marriage was over just as surely as if there had been an actual death. In that split-second of awful realization, his mind reeling dizzily on the brink of a bottomless pit, Daniel at last dared ask himself how honest he was about the professions of love that came so readily to his mouth. Were they words that sprang from a true and solid foundation, or were they merely plaster to smear over the wide cracks that had developed in their marriage?

And more to the point, did he understand what those words even *meant?*

He spoke his answer before he knew he had found it. "We're moving back to the Salt Lake City Project, Rebekah. I can't keep you here any longer, any more than I could keep an eagle locked up in some cage underground." He looked away. "I want us to live where you'll be the most happy."

Rebekah bit her lip. Tears filled her eyes, and she tightened her grip on his wrists. "But Daniel, what about you? This is the place where *you're* happy."

"I love this place," said Daniel, reaching up to cup the side of her face in the curve of his palm, "but I haven't really been happy here. I told myself I was, but I wasn't. I can't be happy in a place that makes you so miserable." He laid his cheek gently against her belly. "I thought if I tried hard enough, I could make you love it here as much as I do. I guess I couldn't, though." He breathed deeply. "Honey, I'm sorry for everything I've put you through. I really am."

She cradled him suddenly, tightly, in her arms. "I love you, Daniel," she said, weeping. "You know that. Sometimes that was the only thing that kept me here. But I stayed. I stayed here because of you."

She rocked him back and forth, and the tears he cried onto her blouse were at last, blessedly, tears of cleansing and release. "That and the fact that you're afraid to go outside, you mean," he said after a few moments, wiping his nose and eyes with the back of his hand. They both laughed, but the laughter brought on a fresh spate of tears, and they clung to each other drunkenly.

Moments trickled by. Calm settled over them like a canopy of silk, gracefully, light as a spider's web. Daniel hesitated to say or do anything more, for this was as close to real peace as he had ever come to feeling, and to break the silence was to risk never experiencing that peace again. But if he meant to keep his word to Rebekah, to this beautiful woman nestled in his arms through the grace of some benevolent god, then there remained a matter to be cleared up.

He tried to ignore this thought when it came, and, when that failed, he tried to push the thought away, but it refused to leave. Like a piece of food lodged between his teeth, it began to irritate him, to worry at him, until soon he had no choice but to deal with it.

"Honey," he said, gently removing her arms from about him and rising to his feet, "let's start getting ready. We'll take only what we can fit in the car, and we'll leave first thing in the morning." He bent to kiss her tranquil smile, and her eyes sparkled as their lips met at cross purposes. "I need to take care of some things with the animals, and then I'll be back here to help."

"Hurry," she said, and touched his cheek, the picture of serenity.

With that image of her in his mind, he scarcely felt the pressure of the sun as he marched through the crackling dead weeds beyond the garden. He was amazed at how simple it had been to work such a transformation on Rebekah. All these months, the opportunity had been right there in front of him, but he had been too selfish to use it, or even to recognize it. He rued all they had missed out on in that time, all that could never be recaptured, and sorrow weighed on his heart. Those were days that had skirled away like smoke through an open window, like music with no listening ear. Those days had flown, like laughing phantoms.

But at least it's not over, he thought with determination. At least we're getting back on track. At least we have something worth salvaging.

And at least we still have our child, whether Rebekah keeps it or farms it out to an incubator until its big enough to come home. Either way, the child is still ours.

Clicking grasshoppers burst out from under cover of the weeds at Daniel's every step, winging away like joyful, colorful thoughts liberated from his own dark mind. Suddenly the grasshoppers were again his friends, and he laughed and clapped his hands at the way they reveled in their freedom. He almost felt like he was one of them. Freedom didn't necessarily follow from a lack of walls, he realized. Freedom was no more that a state of the heart.

When he pushed open the door to the barn, not even the abusive harangue of the Sentinel could puncture his ebullient mood. "Save it," he said with a negligent wave of his hand. "That's not why I'm here."

"Right, and pigs can fly," said the sneering voice. "Eight days, Danny boy? Eight *days* is all you could manage? Why, what kind of sick, twisted, perverse—"

The chickens in their roosts squawked in listless rebuke as Daniel climbed the ladder. His neglect had left them too weak even to leave the stifling shade of the barn in search of something to eat. They had already pecked the barnyard clean. Guilt rattled hollowly in Daniel's chest. Something would have to be arranged for the chickens when he and Rebekah left.

But not now. Later. Later.

A hot breeze stirred fitfully in the shadows of the loft, like a beast half drugged with sleep. Fully corporeal, Allyce sat cross-legged on the floor in a thin splinter of sunlight, studying and rearranging a group of tiny objects. She seemed to be trying to assemble them into something greater than the sum of its parts. "Not enough," she said to the dim heat, apparently oblivious to all but the little items before her. "The capacity of one of these creatures is never enough."

Daniel had not expected to find her in human form, and he lingered at the top of the ladder in some confusion as he tried to regather his scattered resolve. She was always discorporate when he sought her out, and he had assumed that his presence served as a necessary catalyst for her coalescence into substance and shape, as a template for her crystallization. When she lay in ragged oozing pieces on the floor, as he had witnessed on certain occasions, those pieces had to be reassembled and fused together before she could dissolve again into the diffuse mist that was her apparent natural state. Her humanity had always derived from *him*—or so Daniel had always assumed.

Seeing her whole upon his arrival seemed to diminish his rôle in her creation, to destroy a good portion of the magic with which she had always seemed to empower him. She had appeared miraculously in his hour of greatest extremity, on a tiny speck of rock floating at the edge of nowhere—had trailed him invisibly back to Earth and more than halfway across a continent, like a helpless satellite orbiting in his gravity, always available at the inexorable summons of his need. An *attractor* was what she had called him once, as if she were bound to him by more than just the right of conquest—as if they were bound by scientific necessity.

But that was no longer so. This potent energy reservoir who seemed to draw sustenance from his violent emotions actually existed *independent* of him, and it now occurred to Daniel that she could probably assume shapes he would never in his strangest nightmares be able to envision. He didn't know what star she had come from, if any at all, or how long she had waited in perfect solitude on that wreck to be found and adopted by a strange attractor like him, or if she had dwelled there alone at all. Perhaps there were others of her kind still there. Or perhaps he was not the only ex-spacefarer towing an unseen companion along in his wake wherever he traveled.

All this time the tacit assumption that his own unconscious screaming need had called her into existence had been sitting at the back of his mind like an unread thesis—drawing no attention to itself, but quietly grounding his view of reality—while in truth no real ties existed between them.

These thoughts swept through Daniel's mind in an instant, as if some locked vault had suddenly burst open to irradiate him with newly minted facts, as if the world had been altered in the split-second blindness of a blink, everything rearranged so cleverly that it looked no different to the eye but felt wrong all the same. Daniel suffered a vertiginous moment of self-doubt that reflexively caused him to tighten his grip on the ladder.

But wasn't a severance from Allyce exactly what he sought? Had he not come here to dissolve those ties, to set her free like a boat with its mooring line cast off from the wharf slips silently away in the current? He *thought* so. In his disorientation, however, he did not know if this were really so. His intentions eluded him like darting hummingbirds. He tried to tell himself that the ache in his heart was for love of Rebekah, but he was not certain of it.

One glance into the loft had changed everything. One glance.

Not knowing how else to proceed, he clutched at the one route that seemed instinctively the safest—his original intent. He clung to that purpose like a drowning man clings to driftwood, and he let its buoyancy tug his mind back into the realm of clear thought. "Allyce," he said uncertainly, scaling the last few rungs of the ladder, "we need to talk."

She turned her head at the sound of his voice, but her eyes were like windows into a world of ice on the verge of melting, and she seemed to look *through* him into that alien demesne rather than *at* him. Her hands continued to toy with the tiny objects, fitting them together like a miniature puzzle, even though she was no longer looking at them. "These little creatures can store so much anger for their size," she said. "But what is one of them compared to one of us?" Her left eyebrow arched as she posed the question, but otherwise her tone and inflection could have been that of someone commenting rather distractedly on the weather.

Daniel approached her with caution, feeling the warning snarl of the beast from the back of his mind. She wore no clothing, as usual, but as he drew nearer he could see that she was pallid, drawn, and thin, and his incipient lust faded. Her ribs showed through the skin, the delicate bones on the backs of her hands and the tops of her feet stood out like sticks under paper, and the lines of her skull were nearly visible through her face. Her shrunken breasts hung slack. Her lips were dry, cracked, and bloodless. There was no longer any vulnerability about her, any defiance, any allure. She was like a living mummy.

All this evoked no response from Daniel, no pity, no revulsion, nothing—but when the tiny items at her fingertips finally registered on his brain he stiffened as if hit by an electrical charge, sucking in a short strangled breath. "I'm sorry," he said in a gasp, half to himself, and he nearly dropped to his knees.

Allyce was piecing together the remains of a mercilessly shredded grasshopper.

In a strange sort of dual vision, he watched the alien woman before him as her hands performed their meaningless task, while at the same time a curious knot of onlookers gathered about him under the white-hot lights of a sparkling-clean underground passageway in the Miami Project, and as his angry mother pushed through the crowd he was blinded by tears and by the helpless panic of a little boy who has destroyed something beautiful and precious, something which no amount of penance could ever restore, and for the loss of which that penance could never atone.

"It's no use!" he said, whether to Allyce or to the swelling throng or to his humiliated avenging mother he was not certain. "You can't put it back together! It's a waste of time! Don't you understand? It's *dead!* There's nothing anyone can *do* about it!"

"Be calm, Daniel," said Allyce, turning her eyes back to the project before her. "Why must you live in a world of so many absolutes?"

She had arranged the bits of the grasshopper in their proper positions, with leg segments, wings, head, antennae, thorax and abdomen aligned and laid out as neatly as if they were part of an exploded diagram of insect anatomy. She stared intently at the collection of parts, brushed them with the tips of her attenuated fingers. She closed her eyes then, and her skin began to glow with a pale luminosity that Daniel thought at first was just a trick of the diffuse light on her white, white skin. She seemed stronger in that glow, healthier, more vital, with skin as soft and curves as firm and full as he had ever known them.

Daniel tensed, expecting the sight of Allyce in her voluptuousness to provoke a rampage from his savage half, to ignite the ancient flame in his veins—but nothing happened. Relief flooded him, made him weak. He wanted to leap for joy but could not find the strength. The bonds were broken, they really were—if they had ever existed outside his fevered imagination. He and Rebekah could leave, and Allyce would remain, never to trouble them again. Whatever the trick of his will that had tied this alien to him for so long, it no longer had the power to summon her across whatever small or vast distances he might travel.

He was free of her. At last, at long blessed last, he was free.

The glow subsided from Allyce's body, which returned by degrees to its previous infirm state. She spread her arms in a sudden flourish, as if she had just performed some great sleight of hand. The mutilated grasshopper, which Daniel had all but forgotten, sprang suddenly into the air. It ricocheted from his shoulder, hit the floor, leapt again and vanished through the trapdoor, clicking all the while as if in question of everything it took in through its fractured, hexagonal vision.

"So full of anger," said Allyce. She looked at her palms, each stained with a little puddle of brown juice. "But not near as much anger as you or I could contain. Not near." She sagged suddenly, as if her bones were dissolving. "And so much the worse for us. Goodbye, Daniel."

Queer feelings twisted in his gut as he backed down the ladder, and chief among them now was dread. First thing tomorrow, he would take Rebekah and leave.

It couldn't happen too soon.

3.

REBEKAH WHISPERED FOR HIM TO STAY IN BED, TO GO BACK TO sleep, everything was all right, there was just something she needed to check and she'd only be a few minutes. She kissed him on the forehead and on the nose and he could feel her trembling a bit as she said she loved him, and then she turned and slipped into her robe. She moved like a wraith in the faint, faint gloaming of early morning, a grainy black-and-white scene that made Daniel feel as if they were drifting through the frames of some antiquated motion picture. When she disappeared through a doorway that was invisible to him in the near-darkness he sat up in terror, irrationally fearing that it was Allyce rather than his expectant wife to whom he had clung throughout this tender and yet somehow desperate night, and imagining that the usurper was now vanishing like fog at the first hint of dawn.

But then he fell back to his pillow and dreamless sleep reclaimed him.

What seemed like hours later, feeble warmth on his cheek brought Daniel slowly awake. The sun peered through moving gray clouds over the nearby mountains and in through the bedroom window as if both shy and curious to learn what had passed there during the night. Daniel rolled over, wondering vaguely why the window was depolarized—and then was startled into full awareness by finding Rebekah gone.

Panicked, heart beating in his ears, he cast off the covers under which he really longed to huddle for security and swung his feet to the floor. Only gradually as he labored to control his breathing did he recall her leavetaking in what had seemed to be an early-morning dream. Had she said where she was going? He could not remember, but he could remember how she had trembled, and he trembled also as he hurriedly dressed in his trousers and boots.

He recognized what he felt as the unreasoning fear that comes in the wake of a nightmare, but that realization did nothing to dispel his sense of foreboding. Shirtless, in mounting panic, he checked every room in the house, then did it again, even descending to the dank, earthen-walled cellar where pale, blind potato stalks groped up from the dirt as though misshapen corpses were trying to claw their way out of the ground.

He could not find her anywhere.

He searched the house again, not wanting to believe what was becoming increasing clear—that she had gone outside. For some unknown reason she had defied all her phobias to venture into the realm of bare earth, endless sky, and organic materials both living and dead. His blood ran like freon in the air-conditioned chill of his log house. What could possibly have driven her out of doors? If she was trembling when she kissed him goodbye, what condition must she be in now? Babbling in delirium at the absence of comforting walls? Sobbing in half-mad terror at the threat of infection and disease?

Daniel threw open the front door and spun around on the porch. During the night it had rained—an ironic prelude to their departure from the parched little farm—but as the sun rose higher the scudding remnants of the clouds were dispersing. The air was humid and thick, the ground wet.

And two dozen meters away muddy tire tracks led up to the old highway from the unpaved margin where the car was supposed to be parked.

HE HAD OFTEN WONDERED IF TEACHING REBEKAH TO DRIVE HAD been worth all the effort and frustration. An average citizen of the Projects would probably see the inside of a surface vehicle just once or twice in a lifetime—and then as a passenger, never as the operator. Among those who dwelled topside, however, driving was a skill necessary for survival. Most forms of business could be transacted by remote link, but not even the affluent were blessed with food and supplies delivered right to their doorsteps. Supplies had to be ordered in advance, then picked up at a community depot. So it was that upon setting out from the St. Louis Project on what was ostensibly his honeymoon, Daniel had felt it important to teach his young bride the fundamentals of driving. Just in case.

Upon his return to Earth, Daniel had collected sizable exploration, salvage, and hazardous-duty bonuses, on top of his regular four-years' salary. As soon as possible after splashdown, he hitched a ride with a slow-moving supply convoy and headed north. He didn't stay in Florida long enough even to call his parents. He had left Earth a fugitive, at least in his own mind, and now that he was back he was a fugitive once more. He could barely remember what his parents looked like, and he doubted they knew or even cared that he had left the planet in the first place. His habits had always been an embarrassment to them. It must have been an immense relief to them when he had finally entered university and moved out.

He worked his way gradually up the eastern seaboard, finding odd jobs here and there and scrupulously conserving his credit. He spent six months in the orchards and cotton fields of Georgia, and later he stayed for nearly a year in Virginia, where he helped to plant and harvest the vast soybean crop on land that had once been given over entirely to tobacco—but otherwise he rarely remained in one place for long. His travels carried him past the Projects of Washington, Baltimore, New York, and Boston, but opportunities for employment seemed to decrease with every northward mile.

So he trekked inland past the Philadelphia Project, worked the docks outside of Chicago and Detroit, prowled south along the Illinois River like a bead of water seeking the sea. And all the time, Allyce was with him—Allyce, who time and again on the long voyage home from the asteroids had saved him from his own savage alter ego, and who now appeared for him in whatever dark alleyway or secluded stand of trees he might seek her out. She kept him sane—or rather kept the two rival halves of his mind in a state of uneasy détente—but this was all he required as he drifted homeless and rootless across the depopulated face of the nation, in search of something to which he could not put a name.

He found that something in St. Louis.

Most dockworkers in the St. Louis area kept apartments inside the Project—not because they liked it, but because living conditions near the river were substandard and unhealthy. When Daniel discovered this, he found an unmonitored entrance to the Catacombs—as he had come to think of these underground warrens—and sifted through the bars and clubs there in search of tips on employment. What dockhands he could identify, however, were reticent and unfriendly. Theirs was a closed society, and admission to it was granted only upon the meeting of certain qualifications which Daniel apparently did not possess. But despite the lack of success he refused to give up, and it was on his second day of barhopping, in a club called The Dock's Orders, that he found not a job, but the girl who would be his wife.

She stood out from the crowd in that dimly lit room as surely as if a spotlight were shining upon her, but about her there was none of the angelic serenity such a light might have lent her. She reminded him in that moment of a squirrel he had once spied above ground in Miami, its hind legs caught in the grating of a sewer duct. The squirrel was being harried by a pair of hungry magpies, and it was half crazed in its extremity, seeming ready to gnaw off its own limbs were that the only way for it to escape.

Daniel could tell at a glance that the woman did not belong in that bar. This was not a part of the Project that its citizens liked to frequent. She was regarding the dockworkers all around the way she might a roomful of murderers and rapists, as if their very proximity might infect her with some dread violent disease. She looked as if she had wandered through the wrong door in a search for the women's room, and had stumbled into a nest of cobras that had hypnotized her into immobility. Daniel's heart ached to see her that way, as it had ached all those years before at the sight of the poor trapped squirrel. He felt a sudden need to rescue her.

He bought her a drink instead.

Her name was Rebekah. She loved music, art, drama, and literature, Daniel soon discovered. She hated her dull life in the Project, but she had never been outside. Coming to The Dock's Orders was the closest thing to an escape attempt she had ever made. The arts had always served as her doorway into new and more exciting worlds, she explained to Daniel, and just once she had wanted to make her way through some *real* doorway in adventure.

Daniel sat entranced as she spoke.

Rebekah, in turn, was captivated by Daniel's tales of the surface, of outer space—the natural world being the only one he had ever needed or loved. They talked there for what seemed like hours, and Daniel felt a peculiar rightness about it all, like he hadn't felt since his first trip to the surface as a boy, or since first greeting the Earth after four years in space. She seemed to fill a vacuum inside him that he had never known existed. It was wonderful, it was exhilarating, and it was perhaps the most frightening feeling he had known.

Days and days later, never having been away from him for more than the length of a night, Rebekah put a name to the things he was feeling, a name that came as a complete revelation to Daniel. It had never occurred to him that this might be *love*. But upon reflection, realizing that he had not so much as thought of Allyce since meeting Rebekah, he also realized that what she had told him was true. It *was* love. He'd had no way to recognize it beforehand—being so different from what he had once felt for that unfortunate girl in Miami whose name he could never remember—but once it was pointed out to him and identified, he could not deny that love was what it was. It felt as if the two of them, so complementary in their differences, together made one complete person—and for the first time Daniel began to hope, even to believe, that, with Rebekah there, the secret savage half of his mind could perhaps be crowded out and made to die. To Daniel, this was something momentous to envision, for, despite the burden it had always been to him, the eradication of his animal nature was something for which he had never before wished.

By all outward indications, Daniel took this new development in perfect stride, as though loving Rebekah were a part he had been born to play. Rebekah, though, became giddy with the romance of it all—which she had only before experienced vicariously—and soon she was insisting that they be married as quickly as possible and then move together to someplace far, far away. Daniel agreed, bowing to her apparent expertise in such matters. The wedding was difficult but not impossible to arrange, for marriage in the Projects, much like surface travel, though legal, was an outmoded practice not generally condoned. It was simpler for people in love or in lust just to pair up, with no legal obligations hanging over their heads.

Nonetheless, Daniel and Rebekah appeared briefly before a frowning municipal court judge, who, by the authority vested in her by the Commonwealth of Missouri, pronounced them husband and wife with a disappointing lack of ceremony.

Late the following morning, they ventured topside, to where Daniel had arranged for a car to be waiting. It was then that Rebekah, who had never before visited the surface, was confronted by a frightening disability from which she had never suspected she might suffer. Agoraphobia. Fear of open spaces.

As they passed over boundless ground, under limitless skies, leaving the security of the Project ever further behind, an unreasoning panic stole over her. She was nearly in convulsions by the time Daniel was able to get her back underground, but as the panic subsided she insisted that this would not hold them back from their plans. She was convinced that she could face the terror just as long as she was prepared for it. Again they set out, but before they had traveled far Daniel was forced to polarize the car windows and drive by instruments in order to head off another of her panic attacks. So long as the landscape, stretching off to the distant horizon in every direction, remained invisible, Rebekah could control her reaction to it, though it still frightened her to be caught there in the middle of it. The trip was long and slow.

It was about halfway across Kansas that Daniel began teaching Rebekah navigation by instruments. She enjoyed that, glad to be distracted from the low-level fear that stayed with her like a headache. For hours she studied the displays while Daniel quizzed her on road conditions and various aspects of the landscape and terrain. Gradually he worked little snippets of information about vehicle operation into the exchange, relating his actions as a driver to the state of things outside the car, until, somewhere in the plains of Colorado, he judged that she knew enough to try her hand at the controls.

Her driving was initially slow and tentative, and Daniel kept a close eye on the monitors, ready to take over at the first hint of any danger. But she gained confidence as they continued, and was soon piloting the car over the gentle, rolling hills at a steady velocity, giggling sometimes at the surrealistic sensation that came from maneuvering through a computer-simulated landscape.

By degrees Daniel's vigilance diminished, and as they began climbing into the foothills of the Rocky Mountains he hovered on the edge of sleep. His head nodded. He thought to himself that it was probably time for them to pull over and rest, because he didn't want Rebekah driving on the winding mountain roads—especially on instruments, where it was easy to be fooled by the complex terrain. But against his volition his eyes fell shut, and suddenly he was wrenched out of velvet blackness by the unearthly scream of stressed air brakes. Something impacted them hard with a pebbly crunch of glass, the shock jarring Daniel's bones as he grabbed the controls from Rebekah. The car spun out of control. Daniel turned hard in the direction of the skid, and his foot mashed Rebekah's into the floor as he stood on the brakes.

They screeched to a halt facing back the way they had come. The windscreen was cracked, and its polarization had reverted to normal. Blood and tissue had spattered across both the glass and the hood. The exploded carcass of a deer lay strewn down the road before them like aircraft wreckage on a landing strip. The head lay just beyond the shadow of the car, the evening sun drawing glittering highlights from its eyes. The shattered remnants of one antler studded the puddle of brains behind it.

The car still worked, but it took over an hour for Daniel to calm Rebekah enough so that they could continue. They spent the night and all the next day at a travelers' inn near Pueblo, with the drapes securely drawn, but Rebekah's panic would not abate entirely. They set out once more after dark, when only as much ground as could be encompassed by the headlights would be visible, and by morning they had found temporary housing at the Salt Lake City Project, where they stayed on for several weeks.

But from this time on, Rebekah's enthusiasm for her worlds of romance began to die, and Daniel began his slow realization of the deep psychological imprint made by the Projects on all their citizens. It wasn't open space that Rebekah feared so much as it was the threat implicit in what the open space contained. Everything on the surface was organic, and everywhere she looked she was reminded that life meant only struggle, pain, and death. The paranoid hypersterility of the Projects had bred into her—and probably countless others—only a subconscious loathing of her own human body.

The Projects had turned her inward against herself.

But Daniel feared for them both, because, at the scent of deer blood filling his nostrils, he had felt again the stirrings of that beast within him he had hoped would die.

He, also, was turned inward against himself.

SHE HAD TAKEN THE CAR. NEVER MIND THE FACT THAT EVER since that day in Colorado he had failed time and again in his efforts to get her back behind the controls. Never mind the fact that it took circumstances not far short of an emergency to get her into the passenger seat at all anymore. That car with its dented hood and webbed windscreen was the very embodiment of all Rebekah's phobias, and now it was gone, and she, seven months pregnant, was gone with it. What could have driven her to such an extremity Daniel could scarcely begin to imagine.

The ascending sun cast feeble warmth across his face, and in his frustration over the things he could not understand he kicked at some patches of mud that lay slowly drying on the porch. The mud seemed to speak to him like secret writing in some incomprehensible tongue, and with teeth clenched he kicked and scuffled at it, trying to eradicate those blotches which somehow came to symbolize all the stains that had marred what should otherwise have been his happy life. He wanted to blaze like the sun in his anger, to rise and burn away the clouds of duplicity and deception that had overshadowed his every waking moment since childhood. The sun shone in the eastern sky before the fleeing remnants of the night's rainstorm like a promise of the heights he might someday attain, as if the seeds were already planted inside him. To be free to be what he was, without shame or pretense, before the eyes of the entire world...

Suddenly the pattern of mud beneath his feet opened up to him, the key to its decryption clicking into place, and in that flash of insight he couldn't believe that he had failed to decipher it sooner.

He had inadvertently been erasing Rebekah's muddy footprints.

But then, how inadvertent was it, really? Breathing heavily, he held himself still as his eyes feverishly prowled the ground around the porch. Had he kicked and scuffled Rebekah out of his life in reality? Was it something he had intentionally done that had finally driven her away? He studied the ground meticulously, as if that were where the finger of some god may have scrawled the answers to his questions.

A line of her tracks led from the porch and disappeared around the corner of the house, while another led back along the same route. A third set ran from the porch to where the car had been parked. In the first two sets, the footprints were alternately wide-spaced and very close together, as if she had run short distances in bursts of panic before controlling herself enough to walk slowly for a bit, and had then done the same thing again. The set that led to the car was all jumbled in the middle, where she had perhaps turned around and stopped, started back and stopped again—whether in the indecision of confusion or of sadness or of anger or of terror he could not begin to guess—before making it all the way to the car.

Or perhaps she had only paused there to bid the house a silent farewell.

Without a second thought, Daniel began to follow the set of tracks that led around the corner of the house, and it was moments later with some surprise that he realized he was being led through the backyard garden and toward the barn. He stopped. She had been to the barn?

He broke into a dead run.

He skidded through the mud in the dooryard of the barn, grabbed the jamb to slow himself as he entered. The musty, humid air inside assaulted him. Chickens squawked and flapped away in all directions, and it struck him suddenly that he had neither seen nor heard any grasshoppers on his dash to the barn. They must not like to play in the rain, he thought absurdly, but then the harsh voice of the Sentinel cut through his musings with the authority of a hatchet.

"Back for more, eh, Jack?" said the machine, its voice dripping scorn. "Yeah, that's right. I called you Jack, Danny boy. That's your new name, as far as I'm concerned—Jack the Ripper. You ever hear of Jack the Ripper? Yes? Well, I think you're his biological heir—his bastard child, so to speak. Poison in the gene pool—that's what *I* think. Probably some Borgia blood in there, too, and maybe even some Charlie Manson. Quite a *ménage à trois* that must have been, eh, Jackie? Well, your family tree's really showing now, let me tell you. Three times in twenty-four hours. Three *times* you're here! How you can do that and still live with yourself *I'll* never know. I don't even *want* to know, to tell you the truth. In fact, if I had any wrists I'd slit them right now just for being this *close* to you. You make me *sick*, Jack, you hear? Sick, sick, *sick!*"

The tracks through the straw and dirt were jumbled, indistinct. In fact, the entire floor of the barn was crisscrossed with footprints, most of which were his own, and some of which could have been months old. Daniel stomped his foot, awash with despair. "What do you mean, three times?" he said querulously. "I was here yesterday afternoon, and I'm here now. That's only twice."

"Don't give me that, you self-righteous piece of trash. You were here today before the crack of dawn—probably for your morning bloody Mary. Who do you think you're fooling, anyway, Jack?"

Daniel squeezed shut his eyes against the helplessness he felt. "That was my *wife*, you stupid machine!" A cold horror was dawning over his inner landscape. "What in the hell did you say to my *wife?*"

"Only what I'm programmed to say," sneered the electronic voice. "I called you names, and— Or rather, I mean, of course, that I called *her* names, and I tried to keep her from climbing the ladder. Now tell me whose fault it is that I'm unable to distinguish between individuals, huh, Jackie boy? Who was responsible for my programming? Huh? Want a clue? Why don't you go take a look in the mirror—that is, if you can stand the sight of yourself."

"You *watch* it," said Daniel through a tight throat. His eyes had adjusted enough that he could now spot bits of drying mud around the edges of what must have been the most recent tracks, but he no longer needed those clues to know where she had gone. "You'll be lucky to make it through the day as it is." He started up the ladder.

"Oh, yeah? Well, good luck, pal. If you don't recall, I've got a laser here on *my* team."

"Good for you. I may just tempt you into using it."

Flakes of mud clung like small fragments of bark to the rough wooden rungs of the ladder. The chickens settled back into their accustomed roosts as Daniel climbed. He studied the mud at each step like an archaeologist reading hieroglyphics. When he reached the loft, he stood expectantly, feeling as though the weight of his grief and anger must certainly send him plunging through the floorboards to the ground below. Thin, timid sunlight pushed through the walls and into the gloom like an invitation to another, better world. Daniel waited.

The coalescence began almost immediately, but the process was a painfully slow one that took several minutes to complete. By the time Allyce had solidified and the glow had faded, Daniel's fingernails had carved little half-moons into the palms of his clenched fists. His anger was strong, but it was formless, without focus, and as of yet seeking none. He could certainly not direct it against the pathetic creature he now faced across twenty feet of hay-strewn wooden planking. She was even more emaciated than he had seen her the day before, so dry and withered to the eye that Daniel imagined he could crumble her to powder between his fingers without breaking a sweat. Her breathing was rapid, shallow, labored. Her eyes appeared sunken and shrunken.

His fists slowly uncurled, fingers protesting as the knuckles were forced to unlock and straighten, and his anger began to leak away. They were *all* victims here of one kind or another, all three of them, he and Rebekah and Allyce alike—and Daniel felt as if he were dying inside as surely as this alien woman was dying in the flesh. "Did she see you?" he asked, feeling curiously deflated.

Her shrunken eyes seeming to flare defiantly for a moment, Allyce said, "She saw *this*," and, with a shimmer like waves of heat rolling off asphalt, she changed.

For a handful of seconds, not enough for Daniel to get hold

of, she was Allyce as he had known her before—animated, vo-
luptuous, and bitter—and then it was as if she had collapsed inward upon herself again. She coughed and nearly choked trying
to recover her breath, and she dragged in great lungfuls of air,
more, seemingly, than she should have been able to hold. Daniel,
frightened for her, took a step forward, but she halted him with
an upraised palm. "It was an easy shape to maintain in her presence," she said with evident strain.

Inexplicably a tear had formed in the corner of Daniel's eye,
and he gestured helplessly with his hands as he tried, failed, and
tried again to speak. "Did—" he said, and shivered as the tear
rolled down his cheek. "Did she say anything?"

"Observe." Her body shimmered again, and this time Rebekah stood in her place, staring at him with incomprehension
and grief clearly etched into her face. "We were leaving today,"
she said, in the tone of voice she used only with strangers, and
she was pale and shaking, her wheat-colored hair looking black
where sweat matted it to her forehead, her belly protruding
through her housecoat like a swollen accusation, and she said
again, "We were leaving today, and—and he—he always came
to the barn when he was angry with me, and I never asked him
why, but—but—" Then her composure dissolved and she burst
into tears and began backing away from him. "I loved him," she
said. "I loved him. We were leaving today. I had to see."

Daniel tried to go to her, irrationally afraid that she might
back over the edge of the loft. He wanted to put his arms around
her and comfort her and protect both her and the little life inside
her, he just wanted to *be* with her and feel secure again himself,
but even as he moved the image collapsed again and it was only
Allyce hunching over—pale, thin, coughing as if a vital organ
had shaken loose inside her.

And Daniel, knowing that it was too late, knowing that Rebekah and his child were forever gone from him because they had been lost to him from the start, knowing that the previous day's illusion of freedom was only a mockery because it was and always had been *too late*—Daniel felt something constrictive shaken loose inside his own head. A barrier dropped, and he felt the beast rise up from the mists of his subconscious—felt it embrace the rival half of his mind, the sane half, like a long-lost brother. He felt the blood rush to his face. He felt his hands tense and curl into claws.

"You are angry, Daniel," said Allyce, limping slowly toward him and grimacing in pain. "You poison everything around you with your anger and then grow angrier still when it all begins to die."

Together they could kill her—the civilized man and the savage, working together. Mind and mindless fury. Together they could kill her and scatter the pieces so far and so thin that it would take ages for Allyce to reassemble them, if she could even do it at all. Unite. Think and fight, think and kill. Perhaps they could lay their ghosts to rest and then live in whatever peace was possible apart from Rebekah.

"Anger is not a weapon, to be wielded without thought," said Allyce, nearer still. "Channeled, anger is a salve, a medicine for healing. It is to be shared, to be passed back and forth from one to another, renewing and rebuilding. It erases pain and leaves us clean inside. I have borne with your misunderstanding for so long because I supposed that, in time, you would come to fathom this."

Together, his two aspects readied themselves for the kill, knees slightly bent, elbows crooked and hands loose at his sides, poised for action like a jungle cat. She was almost within range.

"I loved you as she did, Daniel, but I have absorbed too much of your anger. It rages within me. It destroys me. It seeks a way out. *My* anger now seeks a vessel strong enough to receive it."

Almost within reach. Near enough to smell.

"If we are to mend," she said, "the healing must begin now."

They sprang, his two selves. This one's for Rebekah, cried his two minds.

And Allyce, in a motion as improbably liquid as mercury, shied to one side as Daniel hurtled at her, seizing his arm in both her hands. She was astoundingly strong for one so absurdly thin. He felt a moment of resistance, as if a rope were being pulled taut—and then Daniel tumbled to the floor, white spots exploding before his eyes as he struggled to regain his breath.

Allyce still held his arm.

After a moment's incomprehension, pain and nausea crashed over him like water from a bursting dam.

"The other woman nurses your anger as well," said Allyce, "but she must find her own healing." She tossed the arm aside and fell on him with savage ferocity.

4.

ETERNITIES LATER, AS THE RED TIDE RECEDED, DANIEL FOUND himself whole again on the floor of the loft. Allyce, healthy, looking the same as he had always known her, removed her cool hands from his brow and rocked back on her haunches, smiling a bitter smile, but with love iridescent in her glittering dark eyes.

He raised his head, heart suddenly racing as the need to flee overwhelmed him. He struggled to rise, but, with a percussive and authoritative click, a black-winged grasshopper landed in a bright patch of sunlight on his chest, and Daniel froze in surprise.

Eyes like black beads stared at him from the dusty orange body—and Daniel seemed to read sympathy in them.

Then the grasshopper leapt back into the air, wings stuttering in flight like strobe-lit bits of a shroud, but Daniel saw now that the little creature was not truly free. It did only what it was made to do, and it had no choice in the matter.

Just as Allyce had no choice.

Just as he himself had no choice.

Allyce stared down at him hungrily, happy and hale and terrifyingly beautiful. Freedom really *was* just a state of the heart, Daniel realized—but it seemed he had given *his* heart away.

He wondered in despair if he could ever win it back.

www.ingramcontent.com/pod-product-compliance
Lightning Source LLC
Chambersburg PA
CBHW022025170626
46808CB00003B/1060